Serpent Loop

Dear Readers,

I just want to say thank you for picking up this book. Some of you have asked me why I write, and the answer is simple. I've always loved falling into fictional worlds and I wanted to create a world for Zane Clearwater and his sister Lettie. I sometimes joke that I hear their voices in my head so it's really good to get them down on paper and have other people hear them too.

My first book *Bloodlines* came out in 2015 and I thought I was done with those characters, but during the coronavirus pandemic, I found myself writing this book you're holding now. It was a comfort to return to Zane and Lettie's world, even as I tossed explosive new criminal complications at them in this second installment.

Your support, your messages, your videos, your reviews, and your Zane Clearwater cosplay mean the world to me. I hope you enjoy *Serpent Loop* and I can't wait to hear what you think.

Lynn

Also by Lynn Lipinski

God of the Internet

Zane Clearwater Mystery Series

Bloodlines

Serpent Loop

Stalked By Revenge

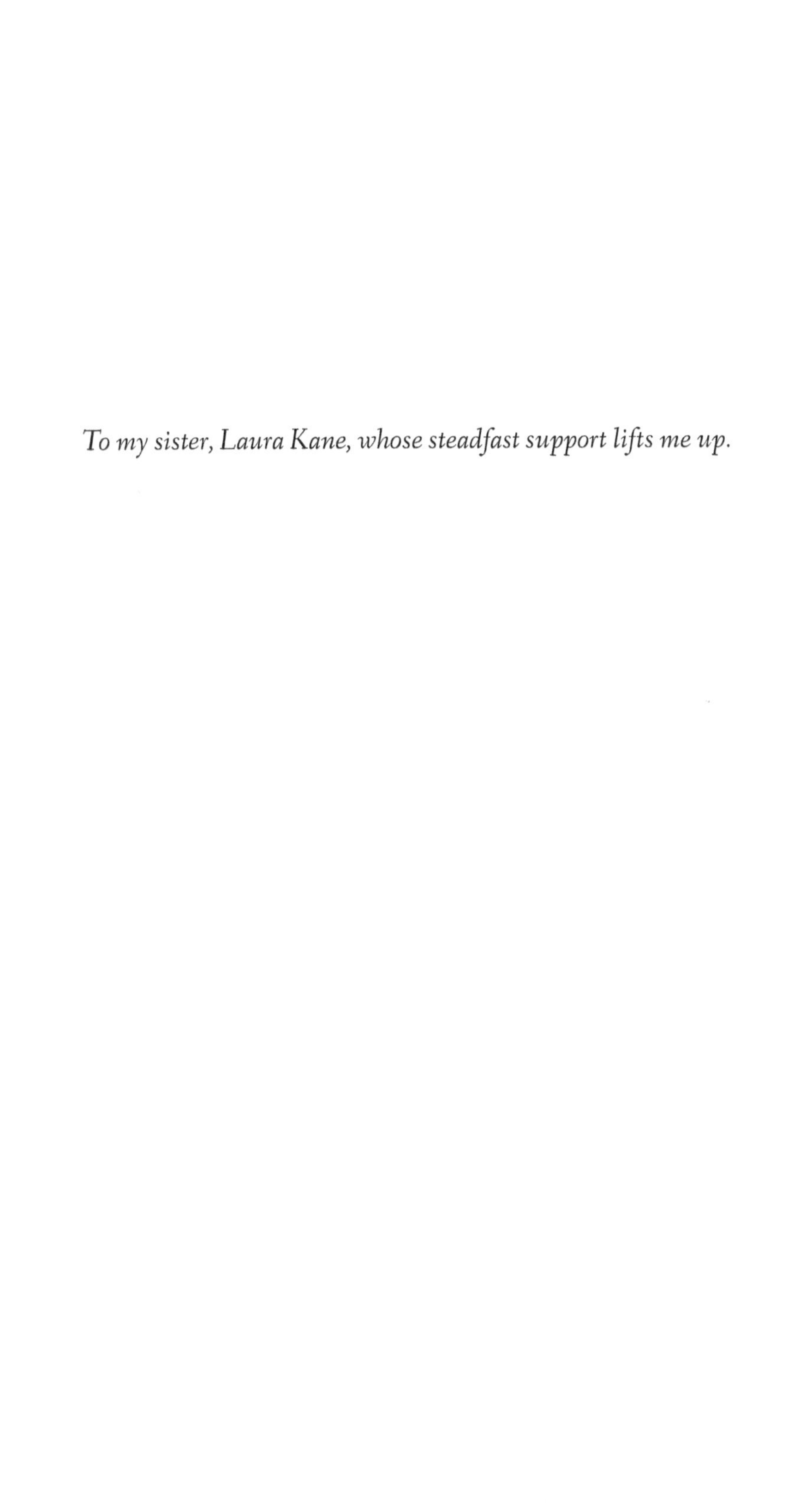

To my sister, Laura Kane, whose steadfast support lifts me up.

Serpent Loop

Lynn Lipinski

Trade paperback edition, 2022

Copyright 2021, 2022 by Lynn Lipinski

Second edition trade paperback ISBN: 979-8-9866288-1-3

Trade paperback ISBN: 978-0-9964676-2-9

eBook ISBN: 978-0-9964676-7-4

Library of Congress Control Number: 2021918974

Publisher's Cataloging-in-Publication data

Names: Lipinski, Lynn, author.

Title: Serpent loop / Lynn Lipinski.

Description: Los Angeles, CA: Majestic Content Los Angeles, 2021.

Identifiers: LCCN: 2021918974 | ISBN: 978-0-9964676-2-9 (paperback) | 978-0-9964676-7-4 (ebook)

Subjects: LCSH Brothers and sisters--Fiction. | Dark Web--Fiction. | Credit card fraud--Fiction. | Murder--Fiction. | Mystery and detective stories--Fiction. | Thriller fiction. | BISAC FICTION / Mystery & Detective / General | FICTION / Thrillers / General | FICTION / Thrillers / Crime

Classification: LCC PS3612.I632 S47 2021 | DDC 813.6--dc23

Praise for Lynn Lipinski
SERPENT LOOP

Five stars. An intricately woven crime drama thriller with a lot of heart.

    —Readers' Favorite

"Lipinski's natural gift for storytelling shines in *Serpent Loop*."

    —Marci Bolden, author, *Life Without Water*

If you have not read Lynn Lipinski, you are missing out! Well written, dark, and well thought out!

    —Debra, Open Book Posts

Lipinski once again weaves an electrifying plot into a brand new, can't-miss thriller.

    —Kayla Harris, television writer

Lynn Lipinski doesn't disappoint with this fast-paced thriller. Her writing is magnetic, charged with intrigue, elegance, and grit.

    —Marina Crouse, writer

Chapter One

It was an April night, unseasonably warm at eighty-three degrees under clear skies and a thumbnail sliver of a moon, no-see-um bugs swirling in cloudy clusters. A sweaty, smelly and bad-tempered crowd jammed the carnival midway set up in the parking lot of the failed Eastside Mall in east Tulsa with its music and lights blaring.

When a knock-kneed drunk tottering toward the Ferris wheel yelled, "Ah, hell, we got a fight going!" Zane Clearwater muscled his way to the perimeter of the altercation because he was working security.

Two drunk men stagger-stalked one another like kangaroos, eyes glazed and watchful, under lines of plastic pennants dangling limp in the air. Hardly the place for destiny to be waiting. Zane didn't recognize either man. That they were strangers and not carnival workers seemed like a good thing at the time.

The fight was evenly matched, with both men roughly the same size and build, but unfortunately, also a few inches taller and more than a few pounds heavier than Zane. He didn't mind a good fight and could take a punch as well as the next guy, but he didn't relish the thought of two angry bulls turning on him. Even drunk ones landed a punch sometimes and he couldn't miss work to tend to a broken nose or worse. He'd already burned what little sick time he had from the maintenance job at the zoo and the carnival was strictly cash anyway. Rent was due and finding that nut every month for the two-bedroom apartment that gave Lettie the space a teenager needs was a struggle with no end in sight.

Still, Zane stepped into the ring. It was his responsibility to keep things from getting out of hand. "Hey! Let's calm it down!" he shouted.

He gripped the heavy black flashlight in his left hand and aimed the beam of light for their faces. The man in the red plaid shirt knocked the John Deere trucker cap off the head of his opponent, then scrambled to his feet and backed up a bit. The other man, wearing heavy blue work pants and boots, got off of his knees and reached to his ankle.

The knife blade glinted his hand.

"Don't do it!" Zane shouted. An ache in his own chest reminded him he'd seen enough bloodshed and violence to last a lifetime.

One man lunged at the other, his body weight throwing him backwards into the crowd. Both men fell to the ground with a thud, but the man with the knife sprang back up suddenly and elbowed his way out of the circling crowd and into the night.

"He's bleeding!" a woman cried out.

Zane knelt next to the man on the ground. Blood was darkening his red plaid shirt.

"You're going to be okay," he said automatically, because that is what you say when someone was hurt like that. But Zane wasn't fully there anymore. He was traveling backward, transported to his father's death just ten months before. The smell of blood, the shock on this stranger's face, the labored breathing. It all reminded him of the worst day of his life.

The day he had pulled the heavy trigger on a pistol and watched a bullet hit his father's chest, the impact blowing him back against the driver's side door of his pick-up truck, the blood slowly spreading in a perfect circle on his plaid shirt. He watched his father gasp and stare and take rattling breaths for what seemed like hours. The father he had just found. And had to kill.

Zane blinked and focused on this stranger's face, forcing himself to know this was not his father. He dimly sensed the lenses of a hundred smart phone cameras shooting video from among the hushed crowd. He lowered his face to hide from them, but he knew it was futile. It wouldn't be long before his face was all over Tulsa social media feeds again. This time, as a good Samaritan, but also a "whatever happened to..." the man who was a suspect in his mother's murder only to find out his long-lost father was the killer. The police had cleared him of wrongdoing, but not-guilty-by-reason-of-self-defense didn't wipe away the trauma and guilt that were his nearly constant companions.

The temporary job at the carnival with its out-of-town workers seemed like it could be a sort of sanctuary, giving anonymity and a little extra money to help with the expenses his job at the zoo didn't cover. That anonymity seemed to be flowing away under the crowd's scrutiny as freely as this poor man's blood was soaking his shirt.

"Did someone call 911?" he said. Several voices affirmed they had.

The man opened his eyes and looked over Zane's shoulder.

"Lettie," he said, and Zane turned to see his fifteen-year-old sister's face behind him, the girders and beams of the giant Ferris wheel rotating in the background.

"It's going to be okay, Wally," she said.

Her words were meant to be comforting, but the look on her face was anything but. All Zane saw in her eyes was fear. He didn't know how or why his sister and this man came to know one another, but he felt through a bolt of strange intuition that something grave and terrible waited around the corner. He was suddenly drenched in a wave of fear, his heart hammering wildly as the wail of sirens grew loud enough to hear over the booming hip-hop music of the midway. The online application for the Tulsa Police Academy he'd started filling out a dozen times seemed like a joke to him. He wanted to help people but this, his first encounter with real trouble on the job had ended in a man bleeding out in front of him, with his sister somehow involved. It was like trouble stalked them. How could he make a better life for himself and for Lettie if he couldn't even manage to stop one death?

Chapter Two

Detective Angus Pastor had a cop's posture. Shoulders back, chest out, still wiry but a bit more silver-headed than Zane remembered. He sat on a white metal folding chair across from Zane in the carnival office trailer, reeking of Old Spice cologne just the way Zane remembered him. It had been a year since he'd seen him, but it was hard to think of him as anything other than Detective Old Spice even after all this time. The only thing missing was the pack of Marlboro Reds in the front shirt pocket. Instead, Zane could see the top of a black vape stick poking out of the shirt cloth. Same poison, different method.

"You look worn slam out," the detective said. "Maybe the night shift don't agree with you here at the carnival."

"The carnival's a side gig," Zane said. "I'm still working at the zoo too."

Wally, the knifing victim, had died in the ambulance on the way to the hospital. Zane and Lettie were back in the crosshairs of law enforcement as witnesses to the crime.

Lettie sat down on the couch beside him, her dyed black

hair tied in a greasy knot on top of her head. A too-small maroon T-shirt reading "Smart Ass University" exposed a strip of white belly.

"Hi Lettie," Old Spice said. "It's good to see you."

"Death follows us around, doesn't it? I bet you didn't think you'd see us again."

The comment was offhand, too casual. Lettie was putting up a tough front, just as she had when Zane had pressed her for how she knew this man, Wally. The look of fear in her eyes in that moment was seared into his memory, right next to the brain cells that held the images of Lettie in peril when his father and stepbrothers had threatened to kill her ten months ago. Maybe she'd tell Old Spice more than she told him.

"How's school going for you, Lettie? Are you thinking about college?"

"I don't know," she said. "I want to move to California."

Zane couldn't fight his impatience. "She used to have the grades for college but if she keeps going like she's going this semester, she'll be working security or mopping up kid's vomit like me." He knew he sounded like a nag.

"Lettie, I have a couple of questions for you both and it'll be faster if I do it at the same time. Zane, you don't mind if I ask her some questions, do you?"

Zane shook his head.

"I'll not eat up too much of your time, Zane. Can you take me through what happened?"

Zane recounted the story, leaving out the part about Wally and Lettie knowing one another. Relief flashed in Lettie's eyes as soon as Zane quit talking. What was her connection to this? His head was suddenly spinning, offering a free-fall sensation similar to the one people paid money for on the carnival's Sling Shot ride. He rubbed his temple and tried to breathe.

Old Spice saw her reaction too, because he leaned in

toward Lettie and pinned her with a flinty cop stare. Lettie started nervously picking at a loose string on the couch cushion.

"Lettie, do you know anything about how the fight got started?"

Lettie shook her head.

"Do you know this man, Wally?" He checked his notebook. "Wally Zittman?"

"I saw him earlier tonight," she said. "He came by for a tarot card reading at my friend Maxine's booth here. She's a clairvoyant and healer at Earth Spells."

Earth Spells was Tulsa's occult store. Lettie had been going there for years to learn how to read tarot cards and practice witchcraft. Magic spells seemed like silly, wishful thinking but their mom had been into it and Zane didn't have the heart to try to talk Lettie out of anything that kept her connection to their mother alive.

"What about the other man? Did you know him?"

She shook her head. "The guy who died, Wally, he bought one of the amulet bracelets Maxine was selling. The kind you wear for protection."

Zane heard the sound of heavy boots on the trailer steps with relief. He was more than ready for an interruption. Bingo Pratt entered the trailer. He ran the carnival with a resourcefulness and sense of humor that usually put Zane at ease. He'd never seen the man indecisive or at a loss for words. Tall and lanky, he had an expressive face and a snarl of brown curly hair usually topped with a straw porkpie hat.

"I got time to talk now, officer," Bingo said. He flopped into his black office chair and leaned way back, staring upward for a moment as if studying the water-stained ceiling.

"It's detective," Old Spice said.

Bingo released his lower back stretch and snapped back to upright in the chair.

"Detective," he repeated.

"Done with us?" Zane said.

Old Spice nodded. Zane heaved to his feet and the low couch squeaked in protest. "I'm going to see Angel," Lettie said in a low, serious voice to him as they walked out. Zane sighed at the mention of her boyfriend.

"Don't you have homework?"

"I'll do it over there," she said. She was referring to the trailer where Angel lived with his mother. The unsavory part of that was that Angel's mother also sometimes *worked* out of the trailer, meaning that she had a steady stream of male visitors coming and going. Not a great place to do homework in Zane's estimation. Lettie seemed to consider the options for a moment. She'd heard his protestations enough that she knew he wouldn't approve.

"We'll sit outside," she conceded. The spring night was mild enough that he actually believed she meant it, even though he was surprised she conceded so fast. Their dynamic lately was automatic conflict. She launched derision in the air and Zane scrambled to keep his temper and not spout off every cliché parent line. *Because I said so. I'm doing what's best for you. Trust me.* Every day it seemed that he found himself in one of those situations with her that no one tells you how to deal with. The kind you get when you're raising your teenage sister by yourself at the ripe old age of twenty-six.

He fell in beside her on the blacktop as they walked toward the travel trailers, parked in the furthest end of the parking lot south of the midway. In the distance, the fabric tent tops of the old mall—now branded the Eastgate Metroplex—stood bathed in yellow lights like an abandoned circus.

"It was hard for me to see that man bleeding," Zane said. "You know, after—"

"I know. Me too," she said, giving him a look of understanding and affection that he hadn't seen since what he thought of as her "goth" phase had begun. Dark hair, dark clothes, dark eyeliner, and the fascination with witchcraft and healing crystals taking a darker turn as she watched voodoo ceremonies on the Internet and special-ordered obscure magic books.

"So, you met that man tonight, at Maxine's booth?"

"Something like that," she said. "Don't worry so much, big brother." For a moment, he felt hope that they could find their way back to being close. But it evaporated as she walked away. She was putting on a front, but he knew when his sister was scared. And she seemed terrified.

Chapter Three

The citrus-bleach aroma from the industrial cleaner clung to the back of Zane's throat. It tasted like a weird blend of powdered orange drink mix and laundry detergent. The teeth-rattling noise from the power washer made listening to music impossible but Zane didn't mind. There was no more satisfying work than stripping away the dirty residue of spilled sodas and forty thousand footsteps off the concrete in front of the zoo's snack bar with a high-pressure stream of water. It was the closest he came to wielding a magic wand. Before you started power-washing, you could look at the sidewalk and think, well, that doesn't look so bad. Maybe a stain here or there. But once you aimed the water stream, the transformation from dark to light was so undeniable. What else did you have in life that was so dirty, but you didn't notice? Something you just lived with?

He was a regular janitor-philosopher. If he were honest, he wished he could make the lingering worry over Wally Zittman's death and his sister's involvement wash away like so much dirt. Ernest Buckskin, the medicine man who saved

Zane's life after he was bitten by a rattlesnake last year, had told him once that physical labor was the best medicine for an addict like himself, one with an impulsive mind and a violent temper. It had been a few months since he had set eyes on the scrawny old man with long grey braids, but he remembered their last visit clearly. He had gone to pay his respects and wound up with advice he'd thought he didn't need but that stuck with him.

"You need to work outdoors every day," Ernest had said, his fingers rolling two hazard-orange plastic beads from a craft project left half-done on the coffee table by one of his grand-daughters. "You need to keep your head under the sky not inside walls."

Zane nodded and cracked a smile at the older man's advice. "I'm not really trained to do much else." He'd never returned to welding school to finish the coursework, finding himself drawn more to a career in law enforcement. Not that he'd had the time or the energy to do more than look up the requirements and print out the application. Part of him was afraid to tell anyone his desire. He didn't want Lettie or Old Spice or anyone really see him fail.

Most people these days, full of self-esteem training and positive thinking, would have rushed in to tell Zane how he could do whatever he set his mind to, but Ernest knew him well enough to skip the speech. Instead, he just returned the nod and released the beads back into the plastic container where they disappeared into the multitude of identical beads, special no more. The thick bristles of one of his grey braids grazed the coffee tabletop.

"Thoughts come to us when we are just occupied enough," he said. "We can find our own stories better that way than looking at the phone." Ernest mimed the act of holding a phone, poking and swiping at the imaginary screen while transforming his face into a mask of fake excitement. Zane felt an easy laugh rise from his belly.

"I'm not on the phone that much," Zane said.

Ernest stopped him. "Everyone is on the phone too much, presenting false stories of their lives and gobbling up corporate fables designed to make you buy more stuff. Our minds need real sensations, the feel of wind on the skin, the weight of a rock in the hand, the sound of rain in the trees," he said. "You're more susceptible than others. I'm trying to help you."

The problem, Zane wanted to tell him, was that he had a hard time relying on anyone for help or advice. He struggled every day to surrender to the idea of a higher power. That's what happened to you when your mom was an unpredictable drunk and your dad was missing in action. Well, until he wasn't.

Anyway, Ernest was right about the physical labor thing. At least today, on this early, clear morning, power washing the concrete outside the Macaw Landing Grille and watching steam rise from the sidewalk like the earth's breath. These days, Zane preferred to work alone, and his maintenance job at the zoo and the security work he'd picked up at the carnival suited his lone wolf tendencies. Around people but not with people. He needed time to think about what he should do about Lettie. That man Wally's death had loosened something deep inside which gripped the anxiety and depression and held it in place. He could feel both emotions descending on him like dark thunderstorm clouds crowding out the sun.

Gratitude check: He was thankful that Ernest looked out for him. He knew that he needed a network of people around him. Taking care of Lettie as a guardian challenged him more than he had imagined. He knew she counted the days until she turned eighteen and was out from under his protection. Well, she didn't see it as protection but persecution. She had called him a fascist two days ago for taking her phone, turning off the wifi network, and making her read her chemistry textbook for an hour. But since Wally's death, she had closed in on herself, hardly bothering to argue with him at all. It made him worry more than the fighting did.

The sun's rays began to stretch across the horizon and the wind rattled through the trees. He flipped the power switch to off and immediately heard the roar of one of the California sea lions, anxious for breakfast. Then his supervisor Gerry rounded the corner from the direction of the sea lion exhibit. The new facility manager's resemblance to the sleek torpedo-shaped mammals was uncanny, like the zoo had decided to hire people who matched the animals. Bald head, a grey-whiskered moustache, deep tan, thick, solid body encased in the zoo's brown uniform. He was gregarious and good-natured and not at all intimidated by the fact that his predecessor Randy Womack had wound up dead in the Komodo dragon enclosure two years ago. Or that Zane's father had probably put him there. His willingness to rehire Zane was another example of the universe slowly shedding some sunlight on Zane's life.

"Almost show time," Gerry said, his voice a low bark. "You know, the two best things about working at the zoo are the early mornings, when it's quiet and you can walk around and see the animals without all the crowds."

Gerry stroked his whiskers with his thumb and forefinger. "I used to work at an office building. Had this financial advisory firm in it. Bunch of hyenas: hungry-looking, skinny, eyeing everyone who walked by like potential prey. Also, they left a trail of cigarette butts everywhere they went. At least here they lock up the predators."

Zane unscrewed the hose from the power washer. "You said there were two things you liked about working at the zoo."

"Did I? The kids, I guess. Seeing them smile."

At the carnival the night after Wally's death, Zane saw a mother drop off her little girl, about seven years old, from an old Toyota filled in the back with clothes and fast-food wrappers. The car had that lived-in look that he saw more and more in parts of Tulsa, sadly often with kids. Cars parked on quiet streets in industrial areas, T-shirts stretched over windows to afford some privacy for sleep. The little girl hopped out of the back seat of this particular car and the woman drove off. Zane could make out the silhouette of a man beside her in the passenger seat. It happened all the time at the carnival, Bingo had told him before, parents dropping little kids off there for free babysitting while they got their rocks off somewhere else. Something about the carnival brought out the worst in people. Zane decided to keep an eye on the little girl, a skinny red-haired child, pale skin looking ghostlier under a slightly too large grey men's undershirt and pair of cut-off jeans.

She made her way to the balloon-and-dart game and Zane tagged along ten feet behind. The girl asked Carla, the woman running the game, how much it cost to play. After Carla told her it was a dollar for three darts, the little girl wrote in her notebook for a bit, then said thank you and walked to the cover-the-spot game to the left where she repeated her same question. After she made her way through all ten game booths, she went and sat at a picnic table and stared at her notebook for several minutes.

"Are you writing a story about carnival games?" Zane said, trying to make his tone as friendly and non-threatening as possible.

The girl looked up, startled. Up close, he could see a light dusting of freckles on her nose.

"I'm trying to figure out how best to spend the money my mom gave me. She only gave me ten dollars and I want to make it last as long as I can."

"Smart girl," Zane said. "Where did your mom go?"

The girl narrowed her eyes. "She'll be right back. She just went with her friend to get some stuff."

Her mom wasn't coming back anytime soon, Zane knew, but he didn't push it.

"Have fun," he said. He left her to her tiny notebook and grand plan.

It wasn't difficult to talk most of the game booth staff into playing along. Carnies have a bad reputation but for the most part, they love kids and seeing them smile, just like Gerry did. The agreement? No one would take money from the girl. Zane watched as she played games all night, finally winning a huge stuffed unicorn just before her no-good mom minus the dude showed back up at the carnival. The sight of that little girl hugging the unicorn in the front passenger seat of that car made his night.

"Yeah, the kids make it special, don't they?" he replied to Gerry. It sounded corny but he meant it. His own childhood had been shaped by all kinds of forces, good and bad, small encounters and small kindnesses that made him feel seen and worthy. Some stood out like arrow-shaped crystals embedded in common rocks. Beautiful, hard, pure. He hoped that he made that same kind of experience for that girl last night.

Zane started rolling up the green water hose. Gerry waddled off toward the restrooms with a backwards wave. Quiet moments like this, before the zoo opened, were when he did some of his best thinking, when his brain settled down and he felt relaxed. He thought about what he knew about Wally Zittman: the Earth Spells connection, the healing amulet he wore. Lettie's recognition.

He let his mind replay the conversations of the last few days. There wasn't much to go on really. Lettie wasn't talking, though he did have the urge to drive over to Earth Spells after his shift ended and see if he could find Maxine and talk to her. If it helped him get some insight into whatever was going on with Lettie, all the better.

He pushed the power washer toward the maintenance room the staff called the roost. Someone along the away had dragged some beat-up couches in there along with a television, refrigerator and a mini-foosball table, turning it a little hide-away. Gerry had no problem with the staff hanging out there as long as they had their radios on and came right away when called. And as long as the bathrooms stayed clean. Gerry had a real obsession with clean bathrooms which earned him lots of fans among the staff and the visiting moms.

Inside, his co-worker Chris sat on one of the couches looking at his phone. Zane parked the power washer next to a shop-vac and two dust mops. Chris's smart phone glass had shattered into a broken spiderweb, and the man was running his fat red fingers over the glass as though that would fix it. If Gerry was the maintenance team's sea lion, Chris was its anteater. Long-nosed, wide-set eyes, slow-moving. Always looking at the ground. He stuck his tongue out when he was concentrating, like he was now.

"Dropped my phone," he said.

"Tough luck," Zane said. There was no love lost between him and Chris but they'd come to a kind of truce since Zane started working at the zoo again. At least Chris didn't call him Tonto anymore.

"You know where I can get it fixed? I can't even type that well into it to find one of those screen fixing places."

"I don't know," Zane said. His sister had dropped her phone a few months ago and he'd told her she needed to save her money to get it fixed, that he wasn't going to pay for a new screen, or what she really wanted, which was a new phone. Come to think of it, she hadn't asked him again.

"The whole phone thing is a racket," Chris said. "You know why they call them cell phones? Because these phones make us prisoners. Get it? 'Cell' phones?"

"Yeah, funny," Zane said without laughing. He dropped into the other couch and stared blankly at the morning television program on mute. Sleek, smiling talking heads. He reflexively pulled out his phone and without thinking opened the Instagram app. The top post, as usual, was Emmaline's: another gauzy smiling selfie, aglow with California sunshine and sporting a hot pink hoodie with the hood covering her hair. She stood on a sidewalk, pointing up at a street sign reading Hollywood Boulevard. "Goals are like magnets," the photo caption read. "They'll attract the things that make them come true. #audition #breakaleg #goodfeeling." He quick-thumbed through a dozen posts before seeing one from Lettie: a close-up of a carnival corndog slathered in ketchup with the caption "so wrong but feels so right."

That reminded him that Lettie had had her phone out that night at the carnival. The night Wally Zittman died.

Chris picked up the remote control and turned the sound up. A woman's voice blasted through the silence about new summer barbecue recipes. Zane squinted at the television screen, watching as a woman in an apron stirred a thin liquid into a glass bowl and yammered about the importance of marinade.

When did Lettie fix her phone? Did she get a new one? And where did she get the money?

Chapter Four

The musty, thick smell of incense clogged his nostrils. Earth Spells hadn't changed much since he had last brought Lettie here several months back to pick up some special-order book. Afternoon sun lit up a display of crystal pendants swinging on leather and silver chains, tiny green and pink and yellow and blue lights blazing. A guy about Zane's age in skinny jeans and brown hair combed back like a 1970s movies gangster ignored his entrance, intent on helping a customer pick between different bundles of sage. His enthusiasm for the product made Zane step closer to the counter to see what the fuss was about.

"I used this white sage after my last break-up. Cleansed that cheating asshole out of the house," the guy said.

"But I want him to come back," the woman said. Zane couldn't see her face but judging from her wrinkled plaid pajama bottoms, tangled hair, and those big slipper-type boots that cute girls stomped around in, she teetered on the edge of some deep mental funk.

Windchimes hung from the ceiling over jars filled with

long incense sticks tipped in brown, blue, red and green powder. Ceramic statues of white women in body-hugging gowns with tall boots and ample cleavage stood vigil around a glass case filled with animal horns and what appeared to be a wooden flute.

A pole attached to the ceiling at both ends served as another display of necklaces and bracelets. A few looked similar to that healing amulet Wally had worn. Zane looked closer and saw the "Made in China" sticker left on one of the beaded bracelets.

"Are you looking for anything in particular?" The guy made no move to come around the counter to help him. He obviously preferred to shout across the store.

Zane decided he'd rather not shout. He stepped up the counter and asked for Maxine.

"She's in the back doing a healing session," the guy said. He peered at a computer screen for a moment. "Do you have an appointment?" He paused for a long moment, his eyes flicking over Zane's body. "You're not another cop, are you?"

"No, I just hoped I could talk to her. About one of her friends."

"Her friend who died, right? Warby something?"

"Wally. Yeah, did you know him?"

"I'd seen him before. Here, that is."

"Did you ever talk to him?"

"Not really."

After a few dull minutes of trying to heed Ernest's advice and "stay in the moment" instead of looking at his phone, a pretty woman with long amber curls and a dress resembling a white handkerchief hurried past him from one of the back rooms to the counter. Behind her appeared a short woman, somewhere in her mid-forties or so, wearing a loose print mini-dress over bare legs and a pair of tall cowboy boots, dark brown with red flames stitched up the shaft.

"Maxine, this guy's here to see you," the dude behind the counter said.

Zane introduced himself. Her cautious frown morphed into a polite smile when he reminded her he was Lettie's brother, which he figured was the best to start the conversation. Always try to find common ground. He had no authority to come and talk to her like the Tulsa police did, so he had to rely on goodwill or charm, and his charm game lacked staying power.

"You're worried about Lettie," Maxine said.

That didn't take a psychic to figure that out, Zane thought. He sensed that clannish, secretive mindset of the occult set, so he talked for a bit about the challenges of raising his teenage sister and how the crystals and spells helped Lettie focus and how glad he was for her to have such a deep interest in something other than video games. At last, her guarded facial expression broke. "My stepdaughter Tiffany was the same way at age fourteen," she said. "She used to say the most hateful awful things. But it gets better."

"It's been hard to keep her on the right path lately," he said. "But something has been off since the other night at the carnival. The night the man was stabbed. I wondered if you knew anything about him."

"He's a client of mine," she said. "Has been for a while, just like Lettie. I've been a little worried about both of them, honestly."

"Both of them? Are they friends?"

"Not that I know of. I mean, they've taken some classes together here. Look, it's probably nothing really. I have an overactive imagination."

Zane pressed her for details. Maxine fiddled with a round blue stone on one of the rings she wore.

"Look, it's only natural that people who come here get interested in some of the darker stuff. You'd probably call it black magic. Summoning spirits, cursing enemies, that kind of thing. They both asked me about it."

"Enemies?" He couldn't imagine who Lettie would think was her enemy, unless it was him. And summoning spirits sounded like a lot of nonsense to him.

"Look, a lot of what we teach people about magic is about channeling what scientists call the body's bioplasmic energy field. Think of it as like the Force in the Star Wars movies."

Zane had never seen the Star Wars movies, a stubborn and useless point of pride. But he knew enough from Internet memes and references to have the general idea of the Force as a mental power capable of moving objects or changing how people think.

"It's a natural force and it comes from us. We teach people how to harness it and use it. That's all there is to it. No bubbling cauldrons and spirits from the sky. But both Lettie and Wally were asking me for more, like that wasn't enough. Something was going on with them both. I don't know what. Maybe you know what it was for Lettie. I remember it started with her wanting to learn protection spells. That only seemed natural after all you two had been through."

Zane had a sharp, unnerving vision of walking into that warehouse with his father, Jeremiah Doom, and seeing Lettie tied up in that chair, desperate pleading in her eyes and fear bouncing off her like radio waves. He had introduced her to that danger and scarred her for life. He couldn't fathom his guilt. He'd sensed his father and half-brothers were criminals, yet like some desperate dummy, he'd told them all about her. Even taken her to the Doom compound. They used her as bait to get him and he could never forgive himself for that. The familiar regret and anxiety monster clawed at his stomach.

"So, what comes after protection spells then? What's the next magical step?"

Maxine gave him a look tinged with genuine worry.

"Hexes, curses, that sort of stuff. Conjuring spirits for help. Look, we don't do that kind of stuff at Earth Spells. We're like doctors who take that oath, 'first do no harm.' The closest we get to trying to control someone is casting a love potion on them."

"Were Lettie and Wally working together on this? Helping each other or asking anyone else for help?"

Maxine shook her head. "The internet, I suppose. Talk about a realm more fraught with danger than the spirit realm. Look, I just hope that if she did get her hands on information like she was looking for, she knows better than to try it without protecting herself."

"Did she say specifically what she was looking to do?"

"Lettie called me one day, telling me she wanted to get someone out of her life. She was upset, almost crying. She wanted to know real specifics about what spell books call defeat or destruction of your enemies. Usually, these spells call upon an evil spirit who specializes in that kind of thing."

It sounded like nonsense to Zane but something about Maxine's discomfort in delivering the information kept him from dismissing it entirely. Whether or not he believed in such things was beside the point anyway. It mattered that Lettie believed. Who could she want out of her life so badly? Anxiety clanged inside him. Maybe she wanted *him* out of her life.

"How have you been feeling lately?" Maxine said. She narrowed her eyes as though measuring his aura.

Zane blinked, surprised. "I'm okay," he said.

"Hold on a minute," Maxine said. She disappeared into the

back for a few moments. Out of the corner of his eye, Zane saw guy behind the counter throw him a look of what seemed to be pity. He'd probably been reading whatever lurid accounts of Zane and Lettie's back story he could find on the internet while listening to this conversation. What Zane wouldn't give to be nobody again.

Maxine emerged again, holding a thin band of woven white cord with a black stone dangling from the center. She held it out until he extended his hand to take it.

"What's this?"

"It's a healing amulet," she said.

Zane continued to hold his open palm upward, the amulet resting on it. What a bunch of charlatans, he thought. Now's the time when she tries to sell me a healing amulet for Lettie.

"I don't have any money for this," he said, shaking his head. "And I doubt Lettie's interested in anything from me."

"No charge," Maxine said. "Just take it. The stone is tourmaline. Good for psychic protection."

Surprised by her generosity, Zane closed his fingers around the black stone. It felt smooth and cool.

"And it's not for Lettie. It's for you."

Maxine walked away and he finally figured out what she meant. She thought Lettie's spells to destroy her enemies were aimed at him.

Chapter Five

Now Zane was really worried about Lettie. He wanted to get home before she did to look through her room and see what he could find. He called Gerry, lying just enough to let him think that he'd been called to the school to talk to one of her teachers. Gerry knew enough about his home life to offer advice about getting to the root of the problem with the teen, which was what Zane planned to do. He didn't like lying to the man. He just didn't want to let Gerry in on the particulars of the witchcraft stuff because it sounded loony.

The Sunwood Apartments where he and Lettie lived looked dingy and rundown in the bright afternoon light. Beach towels with beer logos draped the metal staircase leading to the second-floor apartments of his building, one of eight identical structures dotting the landscape of cracked asphalt and brown grass.

Working side gigs had earned him enough money to pay the extra $150 to exchange the one-bedroom for a two-bedroom apartment, giving them the space and privacy he thought might help repair their relationship. It didn't help, but at least he slept in a bed now and not the couch.

Lettie's room was a mess, with the sharp, yeasty air of his high school's men's locker room.

The sagging double bed was covered in a tangle of red and white sheets and comforter, thrown back as though she just rolled out of bed. Her Smart Aleck University T-shirt crested a heap of black clothing on the floor. On the tray table she used as a nightstand, bright orange Takis chips spilled out of their purple bag next to a tall glass candle with an angelic woman in white and blue. Underneath her feet were the words "La Milagrosa: Lady of Miracles." The candle hadn't burned evenly. A wall of white wax coated one side of the candle and as if at the bottom of a pit a black wick curved over onto itself.

Next to that, a new video game console about the size of a sneaker glinted blackly in the overhead light. He picked it up. Zane wasn't much of a video game player but he knew these portable systems sold for about $150 new, and this one looked hardly used. No one got that lucky at the thrift store, so where did Lettie—or Angel—find the money for this? Usually finding money for fixing phone screens, getting new phones or new video consoles would have been something they talked about, but Lettie was full of secrets and silence and suddenly, spending money. He set the console down, full of worry.

The top of the dresser was the only orderly space in the room. A five-pointed star made of twigs with the ends wrapped in twine leaned against the wall, two candles standing sentry on either side. Lettie's deck of tarot cards had been propped up against one of the candles. A second star, also of twigs, lay flat on top of a straw placemat. Next to that was an empty glass, cut like crystal but as lightweight as cheap glass. A peacock feather curled around a group of shiny stones, including one that looked like the black tourmaline Maxine had given him.

Peeking out from under the bed was a chicken wing, nearly picked clean of meat and skin. It had been there so long it had actually dried out. Zane leaned over to snatch it up with disgust. No wonder they had ants.

The white board he had bought her so she could keep track of her homework assignments was under the bed. He pulled it out, frustrated at the twenty dollars spent and wasted. What good did it do her under the bed?

He expected an allergy attack from a dust-bunny mess but the white board was as shiny as the day he bought it. Its flat white surface was covered in five-pointed star in the middle of a circle. Weird symbols—a lightning bolt, a three-armed cross, a bow-legged stick figure—dotted the spaces between the arms of the star. An open eye stared out at him from the star's center. For a moment, it seemed to pulse with energy, as though alive. Its strangeness felt like an intruder in the apartment and he felt an immediate urge to wipe the board clean with one swipe of his hand, the dry erase ink coating his hands like colored flour. But the artistry of it was striking. The lines were drawn carefully in blue magic marker, the circle as close to perfect as a hand-drawn shape could be, the star—or pentagram wasn't that the word?—was well-centered within. Lettie had taken her time drawing this and he took a small amount of satisfaction in seeing her take care with her work instead of the sloppy efforts he had seen of late. Still, what did it mean?

He pulled his phone out of his pocket and snapped a photo of it to show Maxine, then slid it back under the bed. He would leave everything just as it was. He didn't want Lettie to know he had been snooping around until he was more certain about what was going on. Still, he tossed the chicken wing in the kitchen trash.

Chapter Six

Zane's evenings before the carnival came to town hadn't been exactly boring but they certainly had been routine. It was so much work to keep himself and Lettie fed and the apartment clean, to pay the bills, to wash the dishes, vacuum, laundry, that when he finally settled down to unwind by watching goofy videos on his phone he more often than not dozed off. Each day was a grind of the same, not only having to motivate himself but also to motivate Lettie, something that became harder and harder with every passing day. At work there was an endless loop of cleaning sidewalks, trash bags to collect. It was exhausting physically and mentally. He felt like a robot on a programmed circuit. But the carnival job, and now this murder, had scrambled the code. He thought he and Lettie had been getting on with their lives, but with the mystery of Wally's death and Lettie's seeming involvement in it, his blind adherence to routine seemed naïve and even foolish. How did he not see Lettie's personality changes more clearly? How did he not know she was once again in danger?

He swiped the phone screen to life, opening up the video-sharing app and finger-flicking the words "Tulsa carnival knife fight" and found a website about an endurance race called a knife fight. Not the right thing. He also found two news stories from the local stations about Wally's death. They didn't tell him anything he didn't know already and the video footage was the same shaky, window-boxed vertical phone videos showed the two men while they were still standing. The man in the blue pants throws a punch that misses but all you could see was the back of his head. Then the news stations cut away.

Lettie burst through the door with a huff, backpack slung over one shoulder, cheeks red from the exertion of walking from the bus stop and then up the single flight of stairs to the apartment. He scanned her face, trying to read the emotions flickering across her face. Irritation, first, probably at seeing him sitting on the couch. Resignation, next. She used to want to talk to him, so much so that he would shout to his mother to make Lettie stop pestering him. A prick of sadness as he thought of his mother. If she was still around, maybe she would know the right thing to say to Lettie. She always had a way of cutting through the B.S. and getting to the heart of the matter. She had an intuition for the truth that he used to dismiss as tarot card nonsense. He missed her confidence. He had rebelled against that certainty and leaned upon it with equal measure, like a true north. She had encouraged him to find his way spiritually through his Cherokee roots, though she knew nothing about them beyond pow-wows. She still sometimes had called them "one of the five civilized tribes," an old-fashioned, racist way that people used to talk about the five tribes sent on the Trail of Tears. "You may have inherited some bad traits from your father, but I need you to do the best you can to overcome," she had told him. "I can't tell you how. You just have to trust your gut to tell you what's right."

His gut told him nothing more than that he felt anxious.

Sun glinted through the broken miniblind slat near the windowsill. The room felt tense, the light too bright, hot sun streaming under the door in a sharp sliver, the air too warm. He felt feverish for a moment and wanted nothing more than to close his eyes and stop thinking about what to do next.

He should say something, anything, he thought. Lettie was still standing there, pulling papers out of her backpack.

The question "How was school today" fell out of his mouth automatically and she hesitated just a second before mumbling "Fine."

"You know, Lettie, I was thinking maybe we could ask Bingo if there was any work you could do at the carnival. Maybe you'd like having some spending money," he said.

The suggestion startled her. "Yeah, definitely."

"I know you'd probably like to have some extra cash. Didn't you want to fix your phone?"

Her eyes narrowed before she darted to her bedroom door, which he had shut behind him. "Yeah, cool, let me know," she said, walking past him and into her bedroom. The door seemed to sigh as she closed it behind her, as though the apartment itself was disappointed in Zane's handling of his sister. Her whole demeanor read like a wrong way sign and he had no idea how to help. He shook his head as though it would clear the confusion, and felt another pang of sadness about his mom. This one was about the worries he must have put her through when he was Lettie's age. It felt so long ago, that pre-juvie downward slope of skipping class and fighting and drinking.

He looked back at his phone screen, now a blackened mirror reflecting a dark version of himself clouded with finger-prints. Phones were a sad thing with the power off. No candy-colored interfaces promising endless scrolls of joy, the best video or the funniest post just around the corner. Just a dense piece of metal. He woke the screen up and started a new search: Tulsa carnival murder. This turned up a video of a carnival ride like the one Bingo had called "The Wrecking Ball" snapping in half in India the year before. The ride operated like a park swing made gigantic, with twenty thrill-seekers strapped into the saucer-shaped seating area while the whole thing swayed back and forth. The headline of the video read "2 people die, dozens injured as carnival ride breaks in half." It seemed to him a terribly cruel way to die: On a rundown carnival ride in some small town, a fun day made horrible. Were accidents worse than murders in some way? Both are unexpected. Both leave families and friends reeling from the loss. Murder leaves those who live on with a sure place to set blame. Accidents shifted that blame to the universe, to bad luck.

He scanned the search results again. Nothing looked right. Maybe it was too soon for search to work properly. There was so much stuff on these sites now that it took forever to sift through old content to find the latest. He opened up the Reddit app instead to check out the TulsaSucks forum. Reddit still felt like an old school part of the internet, with its text-based forums and exhaustive message boards on everything from street fighting to Chevy trucks to coffee bean roasting. He'd even seen a board dedicated to mortuary science. The TulsaSucks forum was a hot mess of politics, car fires, storm chasers and the occasional scenery photo of the sun setting over the downtown, but its twenty-thousand users kept it reliably updated on the stuff people really cared about: crime and memes. But sure enough, between a post about exploring the city's drains and pipes underground and another about shipping something called a teardrop trailer to Idaho, there was a post titled "Sleuths needed! Can you identify this man in the blue pants and John Deere hat?" The author "ravenhairedwitch" listed the date and time and the carnival as the site of a murder and said the police were looking to identify the man in the blue pants. "WARN-ING: violent content" she wrote.

Zane clicked play. Nothing but the backs of people's heads at first, then a close-up of long brown hair as the video-taker moved closer to the action. A tight circle of legs in jeans and shorts surrounded the fight. Shadowed faces in dim light. Zane's own face appeared in the video, his mouth open, flashlight a momentary blinding beam. In seconds, the man with the blue pants knocked the hat off of Wally, reached to his ankle for the knife. He paused the video.

Here was the moment of the lunge, the onlookers' circle cracking like an eggshell against the fight, nothing but confusion and the blurry movement of the camera, then the man in the blue pants running away. It was hard to watch. But he did it with a feeling of obligation to Wally, thinking of himself as not just a witness but a witness with some responsibility to make the wrong right. If only he'd gotten there a minute sooner. If only he'd thrust himself between the two men to stop the fight instead of shouting from the sidelines, worried about getting hurt himself, worried about being ineffective. He had been ineffective.

But the man's face, as he ran away, was framed perfectly in the video. He took a screenshot, saving it to his phone's photo app, then re-opening it to study further. He had a round face and sideburns, shiny skin, hair greasy and covering his ears. Zane didn't think he'd seen him before that day.

He went back to the post thread to scan the comments. A bad joke stood out in the mix of generic comments: "looks like Matthew McConaughey after a year of eating at McDonalds." No one seemed to know who he was. But a photo was a start.

Chapter Seven

The Tulsa Police Detective Division where Detective Angus Pastor worked was a vast dark space filled with desks about ten feet apart, most empty of people but not of paperwork and clutter. It had the air of a train station, a place where people gathered temporarily. Most of the action happened outside these walls, Zane guessed, in interrogation rooms hidden from view or on the streets and in homes and restaurants and offices. Overactive air conditioning added frost to the stale-smelling air.

He had called "Old Spice" to tell him about the video he'd found but resisted the older man's requests to simply email the link. He wanted to take action, even if that meant driving downtown and hoofing it five blocks so as not to pay ten dollars in Civic Center parking lot rates. As he watched Old Spice view the video on his phone, Zane tried to envision himself as a detective working out of this room, a man with an important job, helping others by catching criminals. It was a noble idea anyway, even if it also attracted some people who liked the power of the badge more than the service that came with it. Old

Spice had treated him fairly enough. He was one of the good ones. Zane wanted to lean in to the relationship, maybe even find a moment to mention his interest in law enforcement, though his stomach churned as he worried about what the other man's reaction would be. Maybe people like him, with fathers like he had and a stint as a juvenile delinquent didn't really get a shot at that kind of life.

The only thing was that if his sister was really involved in some crime, he would have to be very careful here to protect her. He wasn't sure how much he could count on the detective to join him on that mission. But he felt pulled to help find Wally's killer and along with that, a feeling that finding the truth, no matter what it was, would be a good thing.

Old Spice watched the video with a certain stillness, as vigilant as a snake watching a mouse.

"Yeah, that's a clear shot of his face at the end," Old Spice said. "Now that you've come all the way down here, can you send me the link so I have it?"

There was an impatient cut to the question, making Zane question himself why he had insisted on this in-person exchange. He was trying to control the uncontrollable, attempting to stay close to the investigation to protect Lettie and be a voice for Wally, the victim.

Zane typed in the digits that would send the file to the detective.

"You're worried about Lettie," Old Spice said. His mobile phone buzzed on the desk, probably with the text from Zane. He didn't pick it up to look.

"I think she knows something about the murder," Zane said. His father's voice warning about the consequences of betraying family rang in his ears, but he pushed it away. His father had been willing to hurt Lettie. He was trying to help her.

Old Spice contemplated the idea. It couldn't be a news flash to him, Zane thought.

"You know this?"

The words spilled out of Zane with relief. It felt good to talk about it with someone he felt he could trust. Well, trust to a point.

"More like sense it. She distances herself from me, but I can see her distraction, like she's working something out."

"Some of it can just be teenage drama."

"It's more than that."

"Is there something you want me to do?"

"I'm not sure. I just want to understand her, to help her. This feels like a test of me somehow. But how can I fix it if I don't know what's going on? Sometimes I'd like to shake her silly, make her talk to me."

"Is there anyone else she trusts?"

"Her boyfriend. She's fifteen."

"Fifteen. It's a long stretch, those years between twelve and sixteen."

"I don't know how my mom didn't lose her mind with me when I was that age."

Zane's cell buzzed in his back pocket.

It was a text from his neighbor and ex-girlfriend Magnolia. She had attached an image with the text, *this man was banging on your door, kinda aggressive. He took off but not before trying the door handle and looking in your windows.* The attached image showed the back of a man wearing a white T-shirt and dark blue pants, black hair covered in a red trucker's cap.

The man didn't look like anyone Zane knew from work or Alcoholics Anonymous or around the apartment complex. But he did sort of resemble the man in the video he had come to show Old Spice.

"Take a look at this," he said to the detective. He held out the phone. "Looks like the guy in the video, doesn't it?"

Old Spice picked his own phone off of the desk and pressed a few buttons. Zane could hear the phone ringing on the other end. The detective must be hard of hearing to have his volume up so loud. A man's voice said "What's up?"

"Kevin Perrine was just sighted around Fifteenth and Memorial, at the Autumn Ridge apartments," he said.

Zane's first thought was that the man somehow knew Zane had been looking for him and had showed up to threaten him. But it didn't make sense.

The thought tumbled into his head like a boulder, then sunk into his gut. The man wasn't looking for him. The man, this Kevin Perrine, was looking for Lettie.

Chapter Eight

This was all enough for Zane to break out into a run across the Civic Center Plaza, dodging people with juror's badges dangling from their shirts and people in suits with thick briefcases, carrying sheafs of paper around as though the internet didn't exist. Each footstep hitting the concrete felt like a heartbeat, the iron posts he passed blurred in his peripheral vision.

In the distance, dark clouds moved fast and low, so low they seemed to touch the tops of the trees. Raindrops beat down on the little white econo-car that had been his mother's. He fumbled unlocking the door, dropping the keys on the wet blacktop as thunder cracked overhead. A late model white truck swished by him, its huge tires spraying him and the car with a wall of water. The glow of its red taillights trailed it in the street like twin shadows.

Around him was the unfamiliar grid of downtown Tulsa, eerie in its quietness as everyone hunkered down inside, out of the rain. Down Cheyenne, a blood plasma bank and empty lots covered in green grass and tall weeds sat under a network of powerlines and tall poles, like an elaborate tightrope setup at the circus.

He drove onto the highway before deciding between going to the apartment or going to Lettie's school. Emotionally, he wanted to go to his sister and make sure she was all right. Logically, he reasoned she was safe at school and would be safer there than at the apartment. He exited at Twenty-first Street and turned left, driving past the empty parking lot that had replaced old Bell's Amusement Park a few years back. He had spent some of his happiest days riding the wooden Zingo roller-coaster at Bell's, but it was gone now. Sold to some Japanese rollercoaster collector or something, he heard. That happiness, that invincibility he'd felt back then seemed remote.

Hale High School sat on a huge lot off of Twenty-first Street, a long beige three-story building with the industrial style of a factory and the color of old mattress stains. A blue awning stretched over the three metal doors serving as the main entrance to the asylum, as he and his friends had called it when they went there. He parked in the Taco Bueno parking lot across the street and tried to think the next step through as the rain slowly let up.

Danger seemed to circle closer and closer to Lettie. How could he get her to trust him with whatever trouble she had landed in? She wouldn't mind being taken out of school. He'd make up a family emergency and get her released. Then what? Drive her back to the apartment in the hopes the police caught up with this Kevin Perrine? Maybe it made sense to take her out to their grandmother's house or even to visit her father Roy Magdite in McAlester prison. Maybe she needed to hear from someone else about the consequences of trouble. Verda Davis's little pink house in Okmulgee didn't scream "welcome," the way it was packed to the ceiling with towers of plastic storage bins and black trash bags and stacked magazines, but his grandmother's affection for her once-lost-now-found grandchildren more than made up for her hoarding issues.

He jaywalked across the four-lane street and made it to the entrance just as the first lunch bell rang and seniors began streaming out the doors for off-campus lunch. Or if they behaved as he and his friends had when they went to school here, smoking some pot in the parking lot then heading to Taco Bell as a preventative strike to the munchies. "Watch it, let me through," he muttered to a gaggle of them, all staring at their phones like zombies. Zane elbowed his way inside the hallway. Inside, the floors were pale linoleum, scuffed and dull. It smelled of floral disinfectant and teenage sweat. Flat fluorescent lights buzzed on the low ceiling, washing out the complexions of the students rushing around him. Not much seemed to have changed. Nathan Hale's famous last words, spoken after British caught the officer in the American Revolution spying and sentenced him to death, still hung on the wall above two water fountains: "I only regret that I have but one life to lose for my country." Back in high school, Zane could not imagine caring about something enough to die for it, but that was before his mom was murdered and he almost lost Lettie. He knew now he would do anything to keep Lettie safe.

A brown-haired woman, with little wattle under a thick chin, clicked her fingers incessantly on a keyboard while peering at a computer screen in the front office. Zane guessed she hated her job from the way she glared at him when he interrupted her flow with a slightly timid "excuse me?"

The "family emergency" excuse did its work and the woman dispatched an angular boy in a navy-blue hoodie to fetch Lettie from class. Zane knew a faster way: he texted Lettie to come to the office to meet him. She arrived a few minutes later, boy in the hoodie in her wake. Head tilted, she peered into the office and saw Zane perching on the edge of a wooden chair that felt just as uncomfortable as he remembered.

"What's up?"

Zane cleared his throat. He said, more harshly than he intended, "I'll tell you outside." The brown-haired woman behind the desk had stopped typing and was watching him with what looked like suspicion. He didn't need an audience as he tried to navigate a tricky situation with his prickly sister. That woman didn't know much more about their situation than that he was Lettie's guardian since their mother died, but she seemed ready to pass judgment on his "parenting" skills nonetheless.

He kept his mouth shut until they were in the car. "Do you know a man named Kevin Perrine?"

"No, who's that?" she said, but she turned to look out the window with a dazed look as if she knew exactly who he was and was trying to stall.

"So you don't know why Kevin Perrine would be looking for you?" Zane said, irked by her lie.

"What do you mean, looking for me?" Now he had her attention.

"Magnolia sent this photo." He pulled the text up and handed her his phone. She stared at it with wide eyes. And then she made a loud gulp of air. "He was at the apartment, banging on our door. It's the same guy who knifed that man at the carnival. Now why would he be looking for you?"

"Maybe he is looking for you," she said, handing back his phone. Zane gritted his teeth. The bravado in her voice didn't match the fear in her eyes. Fear that reminded him of the icy terror he'd felt when he saw Lettie tied up and shaking, duct tape covering her mouth, in Jeremiah Doom's cabin last year.

"There's a killer banging on our door, Lettie. Can't you tell me anything? What is going on with you? Are you in trouble?"

Lettie bit her lip.

"I need you to answer me."

He studied her face as she stared at water drops sliding down the car window.

"Is it something Angel got you involved in?"

The car was hot. He put the keys in the ignition and started up the air conditioner, but turned it off again when he saw Lettie was shivering. A group of students passed by the car, Taco Bell drink cups in hand, staring into the car windows, which had started to steam up in the humid air. For a second, he envied them. Their worries had more to do with social studies class, baseball practice or the latest viral embarrassment caught on video.

"You never liked Angel," she said.

That she broke her silence with this tired accusation let him know he was close to breaking through. Her voice had no conviction.

"I'm taking you to Verda's," he said. He started the engine and turned on the radio, hoping the music would smooth the silence between them like balm.

Chapter Nine

Their grandmother Verda lived about forty miles from Tulsa in Okmulgee, a town known both for being the capital of the Creek Nation tribe and its proliferation of dollar stores competing for the Walmart Supercenter's business without success. Verda lived in a neighborhood of little bungalows straight out of the pre-World War I Sears catalog, surrounded by a fast-food fried chicken joint and a used-car lot with strings of tattered plastic pennants and big sign reading "Easy Credit."

She was standing in her driveway when they pulled up, and opened the door with a worried smile, her movements slow as she reached her arms out to embrace them both at once. TV blared from somewhere inside, a game show ending in applause on demand. Zane felt an uncanny echo of his trip here to drop Lettie off before he went into hiding in Jeremiah Doom's cabin, hoping to clear his name of the crime of murdering his mother before he could be arrested. That hadn't worked out so well. He swallowed back the regret and pushed the image away.

His grandmother shuffled her slippers across worn carpet

into her labyrinth of storage containers, plastic bags, shoeboxes piled chest-high on the floor. The corner of a free two-year-old calendar from an insurance agent poked out of a torn shopping bag. She muted the television from the remote in her hand. The smell of recently cooked food drew them down the narrow path to the kitchen. Warehouse store grocery boxes flanked the square dining table. Zane could see about six inches of the tabletop. Cereal and cracker boxes covered the rest. A fork sat tines-down on a white dinner plate, empty except for crumbs and a smear of what looked like yellow mustard. There were only two chairs to sit in: one by the stove and the other in front of the empty plate.

"Are you hungry?" Verda asked. "I can make you a fried weenie sandwich."

"I need to go to the bathroom," Lettie said. She dropped her backpack on the scratched vinyl floor. Normally Zane would have told her to pick it up and put it out of the way but in Verda's house the floor was the only real option.

"It's good to see you," Zane said, leaning in for a second hug.

She patted his back and he felt the tiniest bit of tension evaporate.

"You said to reach out if I needed help with Lettie. I'm stuck, I don't know what to do. She's mixed up in something and she won't talk to me," Zane said.

She pulled away and stared into his eyes, as if trying to read his sincerity. He had broken the fragile trust between them last year when he had said he would turn himself into the police and instead ran away. It hurt to see doubt flicker across her face.

Verda sat in the chair by the stove, her usual place. "I'll do what I can. You want her to stay here?"

"Maybe just for the weekend. Maybe you can get her to open up."

"I'd love the company, I'm not gonna lie about that. I was just going to go to the casino on Saturday but I'd rather spend it with my granddaughter."

"This weekend what?" Lettie appeared in the kitchen with eyebrows raised and bad attitude vibrating off of her in waves. Zane had thought she'd been frightened enough to be grateful. She held her phone in her hand and he wondered who she'd texted, and what she'd told them. He thought about taking the phone away from her, but doubted he could handle the tempest that would follow. Lettie plopped into the empty chair at the table and glared at him. He would need to appeal to the fear he saw on her face when he first told her about Kevin Perrine nosing around the apartment.

"I thought you might want to stay here this weekend, just to be safe, until I can figure out what Kevin Perrine wants."

To his great relief, the resistance on her face visibly softened. "But I don't have any clothes or anything," she protested.

"We can go to the Walmart and buy you some shorts and a T-shirt," Verda said.

"Are you staying here too, Zane?"

He shook his head. "I've got to work this weekend." The thought of working two shifts, one at the zoo followed by another at the carnival, exhausted him, but he'd feel better to know Lettie was out here in Okmulgee instead of at the apartment by herself or the carnival with Angel.

This seemed to settle it for Lettie. "Fine with me," she said.

"How about a fried weenie sandwich?"

"Sounds good," Lettie said. Zane nodded. Getting Lettie to the relative safety of Verda's house reduced his anxiety enough for hunger pangs to start. He hadn't eaten anything but a bowl of oatmeal hours and hours ago. It was already three o'clock. He had an hour's drive back to Tulsa, and wanted to take another look around Lettie's room for clues. He also wanted to try to talk to Magnolia about what she'd seen earlier. It all added up to being late to his five o'clock shift as a security guard at the carnival. He dialed Bingo's mobile.

"What's up?" Bingo didn't sound pleased to be answering the phone.

"This is Zane."

"I know who it is. Miracle of technology. What's up?"

Zane moved the conversation through the kitchen to the back porch for a whiff of fresh air. "I might be a few minutes later than five today."

"As long as you're here by six I don't care." Bingo sounded distracted and Zane could make out of two other voices in the background arguing. "Your sister gonna be late too?"

Zane had forgotten all about talking Bingo into hiring Lettie as a concession worker this weekend. Best to just deliver the news as straight as he could. Maybe Bingo would just shrug it off like he did when he learned about Zane's past. The man had a temper Zane had only seen expressed on others, and he wasn't eager for a firsthand look.

"About Lettie, you know, I really appreciated you're offering her a job and all, but she's not going to be able to do it this weekend."

"Take it outside!" Bingo growled and Zane looked around in surprise, as though Bingo somehow knew where he was. A door slammed on Bingo's end as whoever it was arguing had left. "Sorry about that. Now what were you saying about Lettie? Why can't she work this weekend?"

"She is going to stay with her grandmother this weekend. I think she's mixed up in some stuff and I need her to stay here with family for a bit. Just til I can figure out what's going on."

"What do you mean, mixed up with some stuff?" Bingo's

voice softened, surprising Zane with his concern. He appreciated the sentiment, whatever the source. It was a lonely job, parenting your younger sister. But he didn't want to raise any issues that might get Angel in trouble before he could figure out what was going on.

"School stuff," Zane said. "Skipping class. Nothing I didn't do when I was her age but I know she can do better."

"Gotta nip that stuff in the bud," Bingo said. "Maybe a weekend in Catoosa will clear that right up."

"Our grandma lives in Okmulgee, though, not that that makes it much better," Zane laughed.

"Well, we'll see ya when you get here," Bingo said.

Zane slipped the phone into his left pocket.

"Were you talking to Bingo?" Lettie wanted to know when he returned to the kitchen.

"Yeah, I told him you weren't going to be able to work this weekend."

Lettie went perfectly still, her phone clasped in her hands on her lap. She was thinking she'd lost the job, Zane thought. When he had suggested the job to her as a way to make extra cash, he had taken her "yeah, cool" as tepid interest, but now he wondered if he had underestimated her enthusiasm. He wanted to kick himself. Nothing he ever did was right. "I know you're disappointed not to get to earn some money this weekend. But the carnival stays in town for another two weeks."

Verda flipped the butterflied hot dogs over in the pan. "Lettie, honey, if you want to make some money this weekend, I'll pay you to do some weeding in the backyard," she said.

"Okay," Lettie said. She picked the phone back up and started texting again.

"I'm doing the best I can here," Zane said.

"We all are," Verda said. Lettie kept laser focus on the phone.

Chapter Ten

Back in Tulsa, Zane pulled the car into the weed-and-gravel patch that was his former home, the Majestic Trailer Park. Maxine had said she would meet him at Wally's trailer, which could be found at lot number nine, on the opposite side of where his mother's trailer had been.

Tulsa had its charming neighborhoods—from the charming, artsy Blue Dome District to the elegant homes on Swan Lake to the antique shops and expensive restaurants on Cherry Street—but the Majestic Trailer Park and its surroundings were fundamentally grim. An island of concrete and weedy ugliness, the Majestic Trailer Park and its residents rested in the periphery vision of drivers with better places to be zipping by on the highway above.

Emmaline had told him an old couple had moved onto his mother's old lot. He stopped the car in front of the white-and-tan single-wide trailer, perched on cinder blocks above the piece of earth where he had lived. Where his mother had died. He had had to pay three hundred dollars to have the burnt wreck of the trailer hauled away from here.

He rolled down the window. Not a breath of air stirred, the silence as thick as the late afternoon humidity. To the west an ominous-looking pale steam rose from the still water in the Mingo Creek flood channel. From the distance, it looked like the start of an Oklahoma dust storm.

A sudden blaring honk-honk broke the silence. A white truck hydraulic-lifted off its axel by a foot flashed its headlights into Zane's rearview mirror. He waved his hand in the universal gesture for "go ahead and pass me" but the truck didn't budge. Another honk, this one longer, angrier. He stuck his head out the window to get a glimpse of the driver but couldn't make out a face behind the illegal tinted windshield. And then the driver stretched his neck out the window to shout that Zane was blocking the driveway. He was a pink-skinned man honoring the douchebag cliché of sandy blond hair gelled hair and mirrored wrap-around sunglasses. Zane put a look of apology on his face and pulled the car forward.

Now he found himself with a view of the memorial rose bush Lettie had planted in honor of their mother. It looked gangly, dry and neglected. Brown crispy leaves curled up among green ones like a cancer. He parked the car, careful to avoid blocking any driveways, and squatted next to the plant. It had cost twelve dollars and Lettie insisted on paying for it from her savings. The whole thing had actually been Magnolia's idea. She had found a rock carved with the words "Mothers are love" at some store somewhere and presented it and the idea of a memorial garden to him and Lettie with a flourish so proud he held his tongue about the fact that it was the kind of thing his mother would have scoffed at. And Lettie had liked it anyway. They had turned it into an event, with Emmaline and her parents and a few other trailer park denizens joining in. Magnolia had been right about that little ceremony. It had been nice to add beauty to this space. He and Lettie had still been a team back then. He hadn't known back then exactly how bad it would get between them.

He dusted weathered brown leaves and dirt off of the carved rock still planted at the bush's base and ran his fingers along the capital "M." Despite the neglect, the rose bush had managed to produce clumps of white flowers like small bouquets pinned on green-leaved stalks. When he touched the branches, loose white petals rained down on his head. "Help me out if you can, Mom," he said, as sweat crawled down his back like a spider. His mother had understood him better than anyone. He had resisted her understanding most of his life, wanting to prove himself to be something different. Was Lettie falling into the same trap? How could she not see how similar her path was to his?

Chapter Eleven

Over at lot number nine, Maxine waited for him on the stairs. It was another single-wide trailer on a dirt lot with a smear of green weeds providing the look of grass. When people who had only seen trailer parks as they drove by on the way to their nice ranch house in west Tulsa thought of mobile home life, this place was the image they conjured up. He could hear the "bless their hearts" in his head. A crinkly blue tarp, held down by cement blocks, covered a quarter of the roof. A broken screen door rested against the wall near the entrance, a twisted piece of its frame still affixed to a hinge in the door frame. The wooden door gaped open, a jagged hole about knee-high giving it a surprised look.

"Took you long enough," Maxine said. "Guess we don't need the key."

She was in full bohemian-cowgirl garb. He wondered if it was required uniform for someone in the spiritualist field. On the few occasions Lettie wore something other than T-shirts and leggings, she chose this kind of drapey-full-sleeved look as well. That's why he knew that the skirt Maxine was wearing had what was called a handkerchief hem that would likely get filthy or snagged in a place like this. She held out her hand like a spokesmodel at a car show, indicating he should enter first. Zane felt a spear of anxiety stab the bottom of his stomach. Had Perrine been here as well? Could he still be inside? He tapped on the door frame, a light, ineffective sound that shook the mobile home walls nonetheless. The only response was silence.

Inside, the place seemed worse than its exterior foretold, a dim chaotic sweatbox of particle-board furniture and trash. He felt like he was walking into destruction, an unpleasant reminder of his first walk through his mother's trailer after the fire. The humid air carried a distinct whiff of old garbage in it, with undertones of stale marijuana smoke. Zane shouted hello into the void. Besides the headbuzz of a plane angling in for a landing at the Tulsa Airport, the only sounds that came back were the haunted-house creaking of the floorboards under Maxine's feet, and her soft but rapid breathing.

When Maxine said, "Let's open the blinds and let some light in here," Zane's heart began slamming around inside him like a bird trying to bang its way through a plate glass window. Something didn't seem right. He stood rigid for what seemed like minutes, telling himself to calm down, breathe deep.

He forced himself to follow Maxine through the rooms, his feet dragging through the debris, breathing in the stifling reek. There were piles of dirty clothes, emptied drawers, a broken lamp. A fly buzzed behind dingy white curtains. The kitchen was a tiny space at the back, with a greasy stovetop, scratched refrigerator, and a sink stacked with dirty dishes.

The outside of the home screamed deferred maintenance, but the inside was pure destruction. Someone had trashed the place with deliberate thoroughness. Clumps of foam from the sofa littered the floor like snowballs, and the kitchen knife used to eviscerate it was stuck in the wall. Alarm clanged through him like a bell. Is this what was waiting for him at the apartment? Had Perrine searched his place as well?

"Who would have done this?" Maxine asked. The question hung on the air like the garbage stink. The answer "not spirits" nearly slipped off his tongue but he held the sarcasm back. Maxine was trying to help him and had suggested they come here to look for information.

"Someone's looking for something," Zane said. "Do you know a man named Kevin Perrine?"

"I'm not sure," she replied. "Why?"

He heard a car door slam outside. Sweat collected in his scalp and on his forehead like condensation. Had Perrine come back? With others? Paranoia blossomed wildly. Had Maxine set him up?

He flattened his back to the wall left of the door, like he'd seen done in crime shows, ready to pounce on the intruder once he entered. Light footsteps tapped up the porch. They didn't sound like a man's. A long shadow appeared in the swath of sunlight on the floor from the door. A woman.

Nothing happened for a beat, and then a woman's voice called out Maxine's name.

"Tiffany, what's up?" Maxine answered.

"Wow, what happened here?"

Sun lit the woman like a spotlight. She had golden brown skin framed by thick dark hair cut short like parentheses around her face. As she scanned the room, her full, dark eyebrows were spiked with surprise? Horror? Fear? Zane stepped into the shaft of sun and she stumbled backward on the step, startled.

"I didn't see you there," she said. Country-style accent. *Dint see you.* Her eyes lingered on him for a minute before she turned them to Maxine.

"Anyway, some weird guy in a truck was giving me the

stink-eye out there. Must think I'm casing the joint for a robbery or something. Thought I should find you before he decided to find his gun. But hey, looks like someone else already trashed this place," she said.

"Zane, meet my stepdaughter, Tiffany," Maxine said.

He could smell a sweet perfume coming off of her skin. Her smile tilted up on one side, showing a row of white, even teeth.

"You really ought to get a housekeeper," she said. *Rally oughta.*

"I don't live---" He trailed off, realizing from the widening of her smile that she was joking with him.

"The problem is, I do have one. Do you think I should fire her? I hate confrontation," Zane said. Her smile, the little bit of flirty banter felt good. It was a sweet spot he hadn't found himself in for quite a while.

"Maybe you could have the butler fire her," Tiffany said. "Or you could do it by text. I think there's a gif for that."

"I don't want her to have my cell phone number," he said.

"Then tweet it," she said, and winked.

Zane smiled back.

The kitchen lit up briefly as Maxine opened the refrigerator door and peered inside.

"Look at this," she said. "Now why would Wally keep a can of coffee in the fridge?"

Tiffany leaned around for a look into the kitchen, wrinkling her nose against the stink. "Smells like he should've kept more stuff in the fridge," she said.

Maxine crabbed her hand around the coffee tin lid, peeled it open and peered inside. And then she put her whole hand in, and pulled out a square and thick black device.

"I haven't seen a BlackBerry phone in ten years," she said. "I always liked their little keyboard. Easier to use."

"Let me see that," Tiffany said. She took it from Maxine's

palm. "The BlackBerry Bold 9900. Stunning design. Small, lightweight but feels expensive. Perfect keyboard. But you'd have to be a hardcore techie to want a phone like this these days, because the technology is obsolete. To use it you need to know how to do lots of workarounds. It's basically good for text, email and phone calls, nothing else."

"If he hid the phone, there must be something important on it," Zane said.

"Some people think keeping phones in the refrigerator can stop hackers from activating a microphone and eavesdropping," Tiffany said. "It doesn't really work that well at blocking radio waves though."

She pressed the on button and waited a beat. "Dead battery," she said. "I've got a charger for this back at the store, unless we can find one around here."

Maxine set the coffee can on the countertop and started looking through the piles of junk from dumped drawers on the floor.

"What kind of store do you have? An electronics graveyard store?" Zane asked.

"Kind of. I manage the Cell-Phone-Fixit store on Eleventh Street," she said.

"I know that place," Zane said. "Near the swap meet. Do you have time now?"

Tiffany swiped at her smart watch, candy-colored dots appearing on its tiny face. She stared at it long enough that Zane remembered he had his own obligation to be at the carnival by six.

Tiffany finally looked back at him. "Yeah, I've got time now."

"I'm an idiot, though, I totally forgot I've got to get to work," Zane said. "I get off around eleven tonight. Maybe we can meet up then?"

He really was an idiot, he thought, once the words came out of his mouth. Asking her to meet him in the middle of the night was weird, even dangerous sounding.

"I'm in bed by ten," Maxine said. "So count me out."

A tiny, conspiratorial smile curved around Tiffany's lips. Zane's heart jumped like a puppy.

"I can do that," she said. "I'm usually up playing video games anyway."

Chapter Twelve

Zane blew in late to the carnival, so overheated and grimy that the leftover smell of Wally Zittman's dirty abode clung to his skin. He stopped at Bingo Pratt's trailer first. Nobody else was inside. Bingo was eating some kind of sandwich wrapped in thin paper and staring at his laptop screen, his skin pallid and deep-pored in the flat glow of the fluorescent lighting.

"You're late." Bingo didn't bother to look up. "I thought you said you were getting here by six."

Zane mumbled an apology, throwing in for good measure that he was trying to help Lettie. Zane had thought he could tap into Bingo's sympathy and goodwill from their earlier phone conversation. But he was disappointed. Bingo was all business, just like his starched-stiff cowboy shirt and shitkicker boots.

"I only agreed to hire Lettie as a favor to you," Bingo said. "Then, when I'm actually counting on her to work a shift, she can't do it and you're late."

"Listen, Bingo, I know you did me a solid and I appreciate

that. I'm just trying to get some things sorted out this weekend, that's all."

Bingo turned back to the laptop and pursed his lips. His tongue pressed out behind his lower lip, giving him a slightly monkeyish look.

"Maybe you could help me with something," he said after a pause.

"What do you have in mind?"

"Didn't you tell me you had some friend in the Tulsa police? You know, from your trouble?"

Zane winced inside at the offhand reference to the worst period of his life.

"Not really a friend, but I know a guy, a detective there," he said.

"That guy's death the other night is bad for business," Bingo said. He gestured toward the laptop screen. "Concession and ride ticket receipts are sliding down faster than a turd on a water slide. Bad enough I'm thinking about packing it up early here, but then we can't get into our next spot in Bristow until two weeks from now. So maybe you could ask your police friend if they're any closer to catching that guy. Maybe if they catch him, we can get business back up, maybe place a few ads, something."

An image came into Zane's head of a photo of the carnival's ferris wheel with a headline reading "TOTALLY SAFE." Or even better, a close-up of Ghost Baker, the scrawny, toothless old guy who ran it. The truth was that the carnival looked sketchy as hell in the light of day, but benefited from bright, blinking lights and the cover of darkness. Truth in advertising wouldn't be the carnival's strong suit.

At any rate, business must be tanking if Bingo was considering shelling out some money for promotions. He had heard the man say more than once that setting up the rides in a neighborhood park was the only advertising he ever needed in any town. Excited little kids did the heavy lifting, begging their parents to take them.

"Well, I guess I do have some good news for you then," Zane said. "I was talking to that guy today and he told me they got a name for the guy who did the stabbing. Kevin Perrine."

Bingo nodded and sat up straighter in the chair. He fiddled with the sandwich wrapper on the desk.

"They got him yet?"

"They didn't have him when I talked to them," Zane said. He had to be cautious here. He didn't want Bingo to know about Perrine's likely connection to Lettie, or the visit to the apartment. If life had taught him anything over the past two years, it was to be careful who you trusted.

"Maybe you could call again," Bingo said. "You know, when you get a chance."

"Sure." Zane was happy to agree. "Maybe it would help if the police did a few drive-by patrols, you know, show people that they are keeping an eye on things."

Bingo jerked his head back in a silent gesture. "Dumbest idea I've ever heard, Zane. When did a police presence ever help out business at a carnival?"

"I mean, people with kids, they might like it," Zane said, doubling down.

"You got no business sense, kid," Bingo said. "And kind of a naïve sense of trust in the police for someone who has lived through what you have."

"They did all right by me," Zane said. "But forget it. Dumb idea."

"Let me know what you hear. Go on now, get on your shift," Bingo said. "Early birds are already coming in." He picked up his sandwich and eyed it.

"And let's be careful out there," he said, with a smile,

quoting some old television show as though he was the first one to think of it. It was something he liked to say. Once before, Bingo had told him which show the line was from, but it left Zane's brain nearly as soon as he had heard it. With that, Bingo bit into the sandwich like he was starving.

Chapter Thirteen

Out on the midway, Zane scanned the crowd for troublemakers.

The strings of what Lettie called fairy lights gave the dining area and the carnival crowd a festive look. Short lines of two to three people formed at every food vendor stand. At least one person sat at every picnic table, calling dibs on the rutted, sticky metal outposts while others padded back and forth between stands selling turkey legs, tacos, corn dogs, funnel cakes, burritos, hot dogs, barbecue sandwiches and loaded baked potatoes. Hyperactive kids ran in circles, eager to hit the rides but forced to pause for a quick, unhealthy dinner.

The basic patron was round and fleshy, their attention focused on the binge and gorge session ahead and not looking for trouble. The dress code was redneck workout attire, stretchy leggings and big T-shirts for the women and shiny jersey basketball shorts and big T-shirts for the men. The same kind of disposable clothes Zane bought at the discount clothing store, cheap and meant to be worn a few times then replaced.

Bingo was right. The crowd was a bit sparse compared to the Friday night before. Murder was big news in the heartland and the talk radio fools he listened to on his drive to work had made a meal of it, dissecting Wally's life. They called him a drifter, made it sound like he was a lowlife who may have deserved what he got. The inference made him mad because Wally's life didn't seem that different from his own. Living at the Majestic Trailer Park—they'd referred to it as a "home of last resort for broke-ass people." Maybe it was, but it was his home, or it had been.

The crowd parted and he watched as Tiffany walked toward him. Big round sunglasses sat on top of her head, pulled her hair back from her face. She carried a to-go coffee cup in one and when she saw him she raised the paper cup like a talisman, bright smile cresting over her face. His whole body filled with sparkling anticipation, bright and intoxicating as champagne. Zane found himself looking at her hand just to make sure he hadn't missed a wedding or engagement ring on it.

Slow down, he told himself.

Something about her made him want to go through the fits and starts of a new relationship even as he dreaded the inevitable revelations about his life, his character. The heart-to-heart conversations, him cautious in his insecurities. He wondered if Maxine had laid any of the groundwork on their car ride from the Majestic, asking Tiffany if she remembered hearing about man who shot his father. He hoped she had. He hoped that the interest he saw in Tiffany's eyes wouldn't fade once she knew who he was, what he had done.

Tiffany reached into her back pocket and pulled out the BlackBerry like it was a prize.

"I feel like I'm part of the Scooby Doo gang," she said. "I've always wanted to help solve a mystery."

Her voice was loud, excited, even with the tinny speakers playing hip-hop music and the tinkling music from the carnival rides. Zane glanced around to see if anyone was paying attention. He didn't like people knowing too much about his business and wasn't sure how helpful it would be to have the carnival crew or Bingo thinking he was looking into the murder. But everyone around them seemed more concerned with their food on a stick than his conversation with Tiffany.

He'd only had one experience with amateur crime-solving and it hadn't ended well. His mother's death and the secrets it revealed had sent him on a dark, chaotic journey. He wanted to fly under the radar this time around, staying as neutral and objective as he could. He would keep his promise to Ernest but he also had Lettie to worry about. He sensed she was involved and that his interest in the case could be detrimental for her. He knew he was walking a fine line.

"Are you hungry?"

Her eyes scanned the food booths as she shook her head. "I don't partake of the fried food group too often," she said. "Besides, I'm a vegetarian."

"They have a pretty good baked potato," Zane said. His own stomach rumbled with the yeasty, sweet smell of the funnel cake booth they had stopped in front of.

"I'll take your word for it," she said with a wink. "Look, I've got the BlackBerry all charged up for you now and I brought you a charger too. We had an extra one."

She held out the phone, the long cord dangling from it like a tail. The midway music switched to a dance song, a man's voice singing about not knowing where the journey was going. The song had been everywhere about five years ago and it reminded Zane of better, easier times in his own life. But there was a great yawning sadness to the song as well. Zane had heard the man who wrote and produced the song had killed himself not too long ago. The line about "wake me up when it's all over" had a special poignancy in light of his suicide.

Zane took the phone from her and pressed a few buttons. The color screen lit up, a green wavy plant in the background. A white envelope icon in the left lower corner said there were 150 new emails. He tapped his finger on the screen to open the email but nothing happened.

"You have to use the trackball thingy," Tiffany said. She sipped coffee and pointed to a pad in the middle of the keyboard. "Not a BlackBerry user back in the day, huh? Anyway, you'll need to check the phone out where there is wifi. There is still a basic cell service plan on it but you need to load the email on wifi."

He wound the cord into a loop and wrapped an end around it to hold it tight, then slipped it all in his pocket.

"Anything interesting?"

She drank more coffee, then used the tip of her tongue to wipe away a fleck of foam from the corner of her mouth.

"I glanced through the emails and yeah, definitely, there's something up with this guy. Some of the emails had long lists of credit card numbers, so unless our friend here had a thriving retail shop selling BlackBerry parts or something, I think he might have been into carding," Tiffany said. She paused with wide eyes, waiting for his reaction.

"What is carding?" Zane asked. Beyond the basics, technology baffled him. He had enough trouble with the supposedly user-friendly interfaces of most apps. The thought of drilling down into the codes in the back end seemed impossible. He knew he probably sounded like a simpleton to Tiffany but there was no point in trying to fake it. She obviously was a happy citizen of nerd world so he decided to just be honest and let her explain it to him.

"Sorry about that," she said. "Carding is basically selling credit card and bank account information online. People using other people's stolen credit card information to buy things. The things the digital world makes possible."

"I've heard of credit card fraud, just not that term carding," Zane said.

"Carding is what they call it on the dark web, the place people go to buy and sell illegal things. Your normal web browsers can't find those pages, and search engines like Google don't index those pages. It is hidden but not unfindable."

"Wally didn't strike me as a high-tech guy who could find the dark corners of the internet," Zane said.

"He didn't have to be the one using malware or phishing schemes to steal credit card numbers. He could have been one of the people who tested stolen numbers to see if they work, or even on the frontlines, buying store gift cards with stolen credit cards. That's how they cover their tracks. Some of them buy stuff like laptops and phones for themselves, others buy them to sell for cash."

Lettie's new phone. Zane knew the Blackberry belonged in the hands of the police, and he sensed Tiffany knew it too. But how could he hand it over without at least looking to make sure there was nothing about Lettie's involvement on it? His hand slid into his pocket and covered the phone protectively.

"That's a lot of effort, huh, all that stealing and testing and selling? If only criminals used all the creativity for something positive."

"It's a big business," she said. "You know, some people see it as a victimless crime. Or a crime with an unsympathetic victim —the bank. If you or I have our credit card stolen, we're not on the hook for the bulk of those fraudulent charges. The bank is. So it is a crime that doesn't hurt the little guy. I've even heard some people fancy themselves as warriors against the establishment."

"Yeah, right, real Robin Hoods," Zane said. Even if that was the motivation behind Lettie's involvement, it wasn't right.

Bingo's partner Mike Rooke appeared. Short and bulge-bellied, he wore a leather bomber jacket even though the weather was warm. He began shouting at Zane from twenty feet away.

"Hey, I've been looking for you!"

"One of the carnival owners," Zane said to Tiffany.

"Bosses suck," she said.

Mike closed the distance in small pigeon-toed steps. Impatient alertness shot out from his dark eyes. Bingo may have the hot temper, but it cooled fast. Mike, on the other hand, seemed to burn hot all the time, a personality trait that was not a good match with his authoritarian tendencies. He was the kind of boss who wanted to tell you exactly how to do your job, every minute of the day.

"Anna at the ticket booth wants to take her break. Can you walk her and her cashbox over to the office?"

"Yeah, sure."

"You gotta be making your rounds not standing around talking to the girls," Mike said.

Zane was much taller than Mike. He felt his shoulders slouch a bit, trying to reduce any cause for provocation or further tension. Mike looked like he was itching for a fight.

"Give me your phone number," Tiffany said. Zane rattled off the digits while Mike glowered at him. Her fingers flew over her smart phone.

"I'm calling you now," she said. "Then you'll have my number." With a smile and a wave, she walked away.

"She's out of your league," Mike said. "Her interest won't last."

"Thanks for the tip," Zane said, not hiding the sarcasm.

By the time he saw Anna safely to Bingo's trailer with the cashbox in hand, his mind had chewed over the credit card fraud information Tiffany had passed on. Credit card fraud could explain Lettie's video game console purchase, the fixed phone. But he didn't want to believe it. He walked under the strings of lights connecting the different carnival game booths, white and red and yellow, bathing the shabby plywood booths in an iridescent glow. Beyond the carnival's oasis of light, night-dark trees loomed on the perimeter. The bright white light at the center of the ferris wheel shone like an eye in the dark over the booths full of cheap stuffed animals and winked smiley faces.

His phone buzzed in his pocket. He pulled it out while he watched a guy in a camouflage shirt aiming a dart at a balloon under the watchful eye of his mini-me kid in a matching shirt. His grandmother's name appeared on the smart phone screen.

It didn't feel right that his grandmother would call. There could only be a problem. Zane's mouth went dry and his legs began to tremble. He answered the call, pressing the phone tight to his ear.

The woman named Bunny who operated the balloon dart throw shouted his name but he waved her away. The smiling faces of carnival goers, their relaxed ease seemed other-worldly. He ducked into the dark space between the canvas sides of two booths and turned his back on the midway scene. A dance song beat *oonce, oonce* in time with his heart.

"Verda, what is it?"

Her voice caught on a sob.

"Sweetheart I don't know where—"

"Verda, is Lettie there?"

"Just fell asleep for a moment—"

"How far could she have gone, did you look outside?"

"Thought maybe she went for a walk but it's been so long—"

"Did you try her phone?"

"No answer, oh God, Zane, I just don't know—"

"No."

"Lettie is gone, Zane," she said.

Chapter Fourteen

Three calls went straight to Lettie's voicemail. Zane knew she never checked it, honestly, he never checked his either. He typed a text message with shaking hands "Where r u?" He lurched back onto the midway and started running, breaking apart a mom and cotton-candy-smeared kid, racing past the balloon dart woman who continued to shout his name. He raced the edge of the carnival and into the workers' area, where ramshackle trailers and a few late model trucks sat in shadows away from the carnival lights. He flew up the stairs to Angel's mom's trailer, yanking the door open to find Angel sprawled on the only proper chair in the trailer, his hands clasped around a video game controller and his face washed in blue light from the extra-large television screen sitting on a plastic crate two feet from him.

The trailer was hot and stank of sweat and fast food grease.

"Wait a minute now and I'll be right out," Angel's mom called out from behind the bathroom door.

"It's Zane, Mom," Angel said. She didn't answer, but a toilet flushed from behind thin walls.

"Where's Lettie?" Zane positioned himself in front of the television.

"Dude, come on," Angel said. "I'm going to get killed here."

The shock of his words stung for a moment. How much trouble was Lettie in? Then Zane realized he was talking about dying on the video game.

He wrenched the video game controller out of Angel's hands and threw it toward a pile of twisted blankets and torn pillows, but he aimed too high. The controller bounced off of flattened cardboard boxes stapled to the walls as insulation and landed on a pile of unsorted paper.

"What the hell?"

Zane asked his question again, this time standing over Angel, his face close enough to the kid's sour breath.

"At her grandmother's where you dumped her, dude," Angel said. He unwound himself from the sofa pillows and stood up to fetch the video game controller. The television emitted some sad-sounding burst of chords, the kind of music video games emit when your character dies.

"Perfect," Angel said in response.

"What are you all doing over there?" Angel's mom called out. And then she opened the door.

Red faced and sweating, Mitzi's eyes were raccooned by running mascara. She had the wrecked teeth of a meth addict, angular jawline punctuated by two ears completely rimmed with little gold studs. Up close, her face had a distant, no-one-home quality he assumed meant she was high. Zane assumed she was roughly the same as his mother would have been, in her forties, but she looked twenty years older, sunworn, leathery, wasted.

"Lettie's missing," he said.

The front door opened and a bony redneck with a once-white T-shirt stretched over a potbelly that made him look six months pregnant, stood on the threshold, eyes on the carpet.

"Not a good time, honey," Mitzi shouted after him.

Angel stood in front of the newspaper-covered window. "I just talked to her like two hours ago," he said. He pulled his phone out and swiped at it, as though looking for evidence Lettie was still in Okmulgee.

"Her grandmother says she took off," Zane said.

"I'm texting her now," Angel said.

"Sometimes a girl's just got to get away," Mitzi said. "I'm sure she'll turn up when she's good and ready. My apologies, Zane, I know this place looks a wreck. Usually my visitors don't mind too much, I hope you don't either."

"Doesn't bother me," he said, amazed that she would think he gave even a passing thought to her housekeeping skills. But one thing seemed clear, from Angel's surprise and Mitzi's nonsense, these two didn't know where Lettie had gone.

"Where do you think she would go? Does she know anyone in Okmulgee?" If Mitzi felt embarrassed by her trailer's tidiness, he matched her in embarrassment about not knowing who his sister's friends were. He felt like a terrible brother, a worse guardian.

"I don't know that she has any out there, other than your grandma," Angel said. "I mean, maybe somebody from Twitch or Discord, but I don't know. I could ask around."

Angel had a good idea, to check out Lettie's accounts on the Internet gaming platforms where people gathering to livestream game play, socialize and swap tips.

"You do that and let me know," Zane said. Another thought occurred to him. Maybe Maxine might know something. He texted her too, this time remembering to attach the photo he'd taken of the pentagram he had found under Lettie's bed the other day. Everything felt like a long shot but long shots were all he had.

"She always talks about going to California," Angel said. "Maybe she would try to go there?"

Los Angeles. Where Emmaline lived, pursuing her reality show dreams in some house in the Hollywood Hills. She had moved out there six months ago, drawn by some agent who had seen her on the beauty pageant gown show and wanted her to make Internet videos. Would Lettie really have left so suddenly? Why?

Chapter Fifteen

Old Spice asked Zane the same kind of questions he'd asked Angel. Who would she have gone with? Where would she go? He also asked more sinister ones: Was there a sign of a struggle? Any reason to believe Lettie had been taken against her will?

Zane was gripped by a sudden chill in the night air. "Verda was sleeping, there was no disturbance that woke her up," he said. "I'd assumed she left on her own."

He told the detective about his thinking that Lettie may have been headed for California to Emmaline. A quick Internet search showed that Lettie would have had to get back to Tulsa to either catch a bus, train or plane to Los Angeles. Okmulgee was too small for any kind of major transportation hub. Another thought came spinning at him. She had decided to hitchhike, taking a ride from some stranger with bad intent.

Did she have money? He had no idea. He would have thought no, but the recent purchases and this revelation about Wally's involvement with credit card fraud had him thinking that maybe she was more flush with cash then he would have dreamed. Would she have bought a plane ticket? Old Spice suggested he check with the airport, bus terminal and train station in Tulsa to see if anyone recognized her. But he had one more call to make.

"Zane, as I live and breathe! What's up?"

Emmaline's voice took on more of a Southern drawl than he remembered her ever having back in Tulsa.

"Did I wake you up?" Zane's shoulders tightened around his ears. His clothes were as damp as if he'd been standing in a light rain.

She laughed. "Wake me up? You forget about the time change. We're two hours behind you here in beautiful La-La land."

Zane heard the sound of cars whipping by in the background. Voices talking in the background. Emmaline's glamorous L.A. life as pictured on all those social networks she constantly cultivated came into his mind: private pools with views of scrubby hills, palm trees lining busy streets, the gates of Disney Studios with little Mickey Mouse ears as fenceposts. He felt like he was intruding, but he had no choice.

"Can you talk for a few minutes?"

"Of course, silly, that's why I picked up the phone. We're just on our way to one of these crazy Hollywood parties but I'm so happy to hear a kind voice from home. I'll just stand here on the sidewalk and talk to you."

Zane went straight to the problem. "Lettie's missing. I think she's involved in some kind of trouble out here and she's running to make her way to you."

There was a long pause on the phone line as Emmaline waited for a loud truck to rumble by.

"That explains the call I got yesterday," Emmaline said. Zane heard her voice grow more serious and she dropped the fake drawl. "She was asking if she could come out and live with me. I told her it wasn't a great time. You see, there's this reality show and I'm in the running—"

Zane's words came out crisp with anger. "And you didn't even call me to tell me this?"

"I thought it was all talk. Like she was just floating the idea. I figured it was teenage drama, just like how I used to pretend I would run away."

"Still."

"I didn't think she was serious, Zane."

Zane leaned his head back as though looking for guidance. Stars pinpricked the night sky. She had no way of knowing Lettie really meant it. He might have had the same reaction, had he not known about Lettie's strange behavior and Kevin Perrine sniffing around the apartment.

"Emmaline, do you ever feel like you're some kind of imposter?"

"What do you mean?"

"Like a stupid little kid pretending you're an adult?"

"We are adults, Zane. Hard to believe but we're closer to thirty then twenty."

"Yeah, I know that. But sometimes I get this feeling, that people are going to find out that I don't know what I'm doing. With Lettie. And they'll take her away from me."

"Like child protective services? Is that what you mean?"

"No one gives you an instruction manual or anything. There's no training. Like...you luck into a job, one you really want to do well. But you show up on the first day and the boss tells you there's no training, you'll just learn as you go. So you try, but every hour brings a new challenge, a new thing you don't know how to do, and you're terrible at it. You're in over your head. But you can't quit. And then the boss is yelling at you and so are the customers, adding to the pressure."

"I think that is basically life, Zane. Do you think I know what I'm doing out here?"

"You always seem like you're pretty confident."

"Look, everyone's figuring stuff out as they go, Zane. You've just got more stuff to figure out than most of us. If Lettie comes out here, I'll keep her safe and get her back to you. We're going to work this out."

Emmaline's words had a calming effect on him. Lettie would have a soft landing in Los Angeles. She'd have somewhere to stay while they worked out whatever they needed to work out. Her leaving was just the catalyst they needed to really talk about what was going on with her. He would find a way to help her, no matter what it took.

By the time the carnival closed up at ten, Zane had already formed his plan. He would drive over to the Tulsa airport, bus terminal and train station tonight with Lettie's photo to see if anyone remembered her. He was so exhausted that he didn't try to find Bingo to tell him he had clocked off. He just left.

Angel was waiting for him at the car, a cone of yellow light streaming down on him from a street lamp. Moths fluttered around the light like confetti. Angel had a battered backpack slung across one shoulder. Zane always tried to park under streetlights on this stretch of Eleventh when he was working. Not that his car was anything worth stealing, and not that a street lamp did all that much to deter thieves, but he figured it was better than parking lyn the dark. The street was pretty deserted. Only a few cars were parked on the opposite side and none were anywhere near his own car.

"You going to look for Lettie?" The kid's eyes were wide and he looked scared.

"Yeah," Zane said.

"I'm coming with you," Angel said. "There's something you need to know."

The Tulsa airport boasted of being an international airport because of its connections to cities like Dallas and Chicago and Denver where world travelers could catch actual flights to other countries. But approaching it at eleven p.m., it was deserted. Zane's was the only car on three lanes of road driving into the departures area. Yet still somehow parking was not free. He took a ticket and found a spot in the second row.

"What was it you wanted to tell me, Angel?"

"You're not going to like it."

Zane had guessed as much. "Just tell me. I'm not going to get mad."

"It started out as a fun way to get some new stuff," Angel said. "That's all. We just wanted to buy some video games and stuff. We were just testing cards at first, you know, setting up fake accounts on shopping sites and making tiny purchases to see if these credit card numbers were valid. This guy Kevin knows my mom and he said it was an easy way to make some money."

"What's Kevin's last name?"

"Something like Peru or Perro—Perrine, maybe? Yeah, Perrine." Paranoia hit Zane like a hammer on the carnival's High Striker. Was Angel playing him, waiting for the right moment to call this Kevin Perrine and tell him where Lettie was? He was sorry he had brought the kid along. He was sorry he had been so trusting.

"So do you know he's the guy who killed Wally Zittman at the carnival last week?"

"Yeah, that's what I heard," Angel said. One corner of his mouth lifted in a watery smile.

"Lettie knew this too?" The image of Lettie biting her lip, staring out the window of the car in front of the high school. Zane grew worried, first about her, then about himself.

"Look, I really care about Lettie. I mean—" Angel was stammering now. "I love her. I don't want anything to happen to her."

"Yeah." Zane relaxed just a fraction. The kid's depth of feeling for Lettie was clear. Maybe he could trust him. What was that phrase people used—trust but verify? That was the tack he would take with Angel. Cautious trust. "We're on the same side there, Angel. We've just got to find out where she went and make sure she's safe."

"Yeah." Angel pulled his phone out of his pocket. His hands trembled a bit as he swiped at the screen for a message. "It's just my mom," he said. "I thought it might be Lettie."

Inside, the airport felt even more deserted than the outside had. Not even a janitor could be found polishing the floors or emptying out trash cans. The ticket counter with the airline logos was well-lit but empty. It was like trying to find a cashier at the CVS Drug Store. It was as though every employee went into hiding when the front door opened. Stripped of sound other than their feet on the polished floor tiles, the airport felt cavernous, eerie.

A black board showing departures and arrivals showed just about twenty flights coming in and out of the airport every day. None went to Los Angeles, and the last flight out took place at eight-thirty at night. Zane did some quick mental math. Lettie would not have had enough time to get to Tulsa from Okmulgee, buy a ticket and take off. She'd gone missing probably about seven or so, though it was hard to know for sure since Verda had been asleep.

"This feels like a dead end for now," Zane said. "Let's check out the bus station."

Angel was peering at his phone screen. "The Greyhound website says the station's hours are nine a.m. to four-thirty."

Zane felt deflated, his shoulder sagging for a moment as he considered his options. They weren't going to find her tonight.

"Let's text her one more time, me and you. Tell her she's not in any trouble, I just want to help her stay safe, okay, Angel?"

Angel's phone pinged as if it heard them talking.

"Is that from Lettie?"

Angel stared at his phone like a zombie before shaking his head. "It's from *them*."

The way Angel said them there was only one meaning for it. It had to be the guys running the credit card ring.

Tell him to come to Bamboozle's Showgirls. It's about Lettie.

Zane knew the place. It was off Memorial Avenue in an L-shaped shopping center with a used children's furniture store, a mom-and-pop donut shop, and a thriving medical marijuana dispensary, courtesy of Oklahoma making it legal as of 2018. Meeting these criminals at a strip club was a sordid prospect, underscoring his worst fears for his sister. After the mess with Jeremiah Doom, he didn't want anything to do with people like this, except maybe as law enforcement keeping them in line. What on earth motivated Lettie to get mixed up with these people?

Chapter Sixteen

There's something sad about a strip mall at night in Tulsa, empty parking lot dotted in yellow-orange cones of light, big broad spaces clearly intended for crowds of people, but in practice utilized by few. A story of high expectations and low reality.

At the far end, near a dialysis place and a daycare for adults with memory problems, about ten late-model trucks were parked crooked as though no lines had been painted on the blacktop, taking up multiple spaces that seemed selfish and aggressive despite the fact that space was clearly not a problem. Zane parked within slanted parking spot lines himself, setting an example no one would pay any attention to. Maybe he should take a clue from their parking anyway. They didn't have door dings all over their precious modes of transportation like he did.

"I guess you'll have to stay in the car," Zane said.

"Why is that?"

"You gotta be 21 to go in a place like this."

Angel laughed. "Oh, I've been there before. More than once. It's not a big deal."

And I thought I had a rough childhood, Zane thought. Angel's mother probably took him to this place or at least introduced him to the people who invited him here tonight. He felt sorry for the teen. Still, Zane was close enough to his own high school years to remember how he and his friends tried to get into another strip club called Lady Godiva's once or twice. It had been like a badge of honor, something to brag about to the other guys at school.

Another look at Angel and he knew that wasn't the case for him. Angel might be kind of dumb to have fallen into this situation, but Zane could tell he was good at heart. His affection for Lettie shone crystal clear and he was enough of a video gamer that he'd be more likely to brag about wins on Rocketleague instead of some sordid club like this.

Bamboozles was at the far end of the L-shaped center. The glass windows in the front had been painted a matte black paint, and a neon sign blinked and buzzed, reading Adults Only.

Zane pushed through the front door with more confidence than he felt. He had the sense of walking into an underground cave. Traffic noise from the highway faded, and the world shrank to cool air and dim light. The only sound was bone-quaking bass emitting from a set of huge speakers mounted on the wall.

He scanned the room, hyperaware that he was being checked out. He wrenched his shoulders back to appear taller and leaned over to shout into Angel's ear, "Who are we looking for?"

"I don't see them yet," Angel said.

The urge for a drink struck Zane hard. Even with six months sober, the thirst remained the same. The longing for the warmth on the back of the throat, the flush of contentment, however temporary, the promise of oblivion, a bad day blotted out. He made himself play the fantasy all the way through: too many drinks chasing that elusive good feeling, the passing out, the banging head, cottony mouth, shame of lack of willpower, broken promises. Never mind.

The bar had two rooms. The first, where they stood, was small, with a bar and about ten tiny tables. The second room was larger, holding a stage and more tables, and one long bar running the length of one wall. Men filled a line of stools, faces turned to the stage. Next to the stage was a doorway with a curtain instead of a door, marked Backstage.

On the stage a spotlight illuminated a woman bumping and grinding to a rap song: *taste, taste, she can get a taste.* She had long pink hair and wore thigh-high patent leather boots, black panties and what looked like a Sanskrit tattoo on her chest.

"That's Kayleigh on stage," Angel said. "She's supergood at Fortnite."

Leave it to Angel to admire the woman for her video game prowess and not for her looks or dancing skills. He was starting to really like him.

"She looks like she has quick reflexes," Zane said. At first he thought she was older than him, somewhere in her mid-thirties, but as they moved closer he could see was young, probably early twenties or so. She just had the makeup and fake eyelashes caked on so thick she looked older.

The room's focus was aimed the stage, and so were the wolf whistles and shouts. A ragged cheer went up as Kayleigh spun around the chrome pole, breasts flying. Zane wrested his attention away. He had to stay focused and also there was something a little sad about the performance, as though Kayleigh wished she were battling bad guys in Fortnite and not twirling her body in front of a bunch of sloppy drunks in a strip club. Or maybe he was projecting that on to her. He knew *he* didn't want to be there.

He was the only one, though. The bar's patrons seemed lusty and untroubled, a troop of chimpanzees in the jungle, whistling, clapping, staring. They were here to party and forget their troubles. And no one seemed to have a guilty conscience. Get drunk tonight and let off some steam. Go home to bed, wake up hungover, mow the lawn, barbecue with the family, go to church, whatever folks did that populated their social media feeds. The respectable stuff. The American family stuff. Five days of work and two days off, predictable.

As a teen Zane had cultivated an outsider's persona, never feeling like he fit in and deciding to embrace it. But tonight he wanted to be a part of the regular community. Part of that beautiful oblivion. There was a beauty and a stability in the sameness of routine. What sort of curse did he have that put him in a strip club meeting some gangster while his sister was missing?

The song ended and the woman went behind the curtain. Almost immediately, a big dude with razor-sharp blond spikes for hair emerged from the same spot. He wore cowboy boots and jeans with a huge belt buckle, tight black T-shirt on top.

Zane watched him move across the room toward them. It was easy to track him through the crowd and not just because he was a foot taller than anyone else in the room. People parted for him like Moses through the Red Sea. He looked tough, not someone you wanted to test to find out what he'd do.

Lettie was in trouble, Zane thought. This guy looks serious.

The man lifted his cheeks in a fake smile. "Let's chat," he said. "Can I get you a drink?"

Zane shook his head. He definitely needed to be sober for this guy and he didn't want to owe him one thing, not even a soft drink.

"Yeah, I'm Zane. What's your name?"

The man stared back at him and Angel rushed to fill the silence. "This is Gene," he said.

"Why don't you go enjoy the show, Angel?" Gene said, even though no dancer was on the stage. Zane felt a stab of anxiety. He had allowed Angel to lure him here and now what? What had he gotten into?

Angel left the table with reluctance. Zane wasn't sure if it was caused by guilt or fear. Maybe both. Still, this was the path they were on. He had to walk through it now.

Gene sat in the chair Angel vacated. "Your sister has something of mine."

Gene's eyes were as flat as the black-painted walls around them.

"I want my property back," he said.

The music and hooting in the bar leveled into a buzz, which Zane realized was the sound of the blood pounding in his ears. A rush of fear washed through him. What had Lettie done?

"I don't know anything about it," he said.

"She thinks she's going to blackmail us," Gene said. "You and me both know she's in over her head."

That much seemed clear, Zane thought.

"So I'm gonna cut her some slack," Gene said. "She's a kid. But you're not. I hold you responsible." His tongue worked the bottoms of his upper teeth while he let the words sink in.

"Get my property back and tell her to keep her mouth shut, and everything will be fine."

Zane knew enough from his interactions with his father not to show any fear. This guy would feed off any energy he offered.

"And what guarantee do I have of that?" Zane said.

The man leaned back in the chair with a grim smile. "You don't have no choice," he said.

Gene sat up a little straighter, and his eyes settled on the door like a snake poised to strike. Then they switched back to Zane.

"Are you a dumbshit?"

The self-deprecating part of Zane wanted to agree. Why yes, I am a dumbshit, sitting here with you in another stupid mess, but he knew a threat when he heard it. And he also knew not to back down.

"What do you mean by that?"

"You tell the cops to show up?" And he jerked a thumb toward the front.

Relief spread through Zane, almost as intoxicating as a beer would have been. It was like hearing the cavalry had arrived.

He turned around to see Old Spice at the door. But the patrons seemed unbothered by the sight of the detective.

A hand clapped down on the table and he craned his neck up to see Old Spice's face, pointed at Gene.

"Look at you with a nice packed house," Pastor said. "Business looks good."

Gene produced another of his smile-not-smiles. "You betcha. Can I buy you a drink, Detective Pastor?" He emphasized the detective part so it sounded like a sneer.

Pastor ignored the question and the sneer. If he was surprised to see Zane there, he didn't show it.

"I'm sure you're just trying to help out here with this one's missing sister, right? Out of kindness?"

"Zeb here has a missing sister? That's terrible, Zeb," Gene said.

"It's Zane."

Gene hesitated just long enough to register a silent "whatever" to the correction.

"I'm sure you don't know where Kevin Perrine is either, do you?" Pastor said.

"Haven't seen him."

"Of course not." Old Spice's mouth twisted skeptically.

"I haven't seen him for days."

"I'm sure you'd tell me if you had."

"We always cooperate fully with the police. I'm a businessman."

It was ridiculous timing for Perrine to emerge from the draped entrance by the stage with a small, dark-haired woman in a white bikini. Old Spice saw him too.

Zane stood up and followed Old Spice as he moved the close the space between them. Gene, unaware that Perrine had appeared, turned around to see what their focus was on.

Perrine did a hasty 180, barging away from them through a large group, accidentally slamming the back of a customer. A beer slipped out of his hands, exploding on the floor.

Zane picked up his pace to match the detective's. Someone stepped in his path and he almost stumbled over them in his rush.

"Excuse me," he said.

"This way, Zane." It was Angel. "Follow me."

Angel cut sharply left, elbowing through the crowd. He seemed to be heading straight for a blank wall.

There was no visible door that Zane could see, but Angel pushed his hand into a poster of a bare-breasted woman on a motorcycle and the wall gave way to a regular, rectangular door which led into a long corridor with industrial tile floor and fluorescent lights.

Zane glanced over his shoulder and saw Gene pushing aggressively through the crowd, his phone pressed to his ear. He let the door slam behind him and followed Angel down to two metal doors visible at the end.

"This goes to the parking lot," Angel said.

They charged through the doors into the parking lot at the

back of the center, on the opposite side of where customers parked. A white econo-car rocked in front of them, a man in the driver's seat with his head thrown back and his eyes shut, a glint of blonde hair in his lap. It was a poorly lit loading area, a large container marked "Medical Waste" and a smattering of beat-up old cars and two silver Ford pickups.

"Which one is his car?"

"I don't know," Angel said.

The sound of an engine firing up answered the question. Two headlights burst to life on a brown Subaru. Old Spice came running through a different door than Zane and Angel had exited, breathing hard. His light blue polo shirt had a big wet spot on the front of it, as if someone had thrown a drink at him.

Perrine executed a squealing three-point turn and sped away.

"Damn," Old Spice muttered. "We should have had a car sitting on this place." He started tapping and swiping at his phone.

"And what in the hell are you playing at, Zane?" he said. "These people are serious trouble. It's like you don't have any sense even after everything that has happened. What you got, a death wish?" The detective kicked a piece of junk metal and it skittered across the pavement.

The detective's words stabbed at Zane's gut. *Let him think what he wants.* Zane would do whatever it took to get his sister home safely.

Chapter Seventeen

It was mid-morning, the sunlight glowing softly through the slats of the miniblinds of Zane's bedroom.

He jerked awake at the sound of the phone three inches from his head. He pulled himself up on one elbow and hit the button to accept the call. Emmaline's voice sounded tinny and far away through the phone's speaker.

Angel came running from the living room, where he'd slept. He stood in the doorway with a fleece throw wrapped around his shoulders like he was cold.

"Did you hear from Lettie?" Emmaline said.

"No, have you?"

"No, I just woke up thinking about her, worried."

"We should be worried about her. She's mixed up in some kind of credit card fraud thing and she took something from one of them. He wants it back."

"Oh shit."

"Yeah. I've got her boyfriend with me. We're going to ask around at the bus station and the airport. We tried the airport last night but no one was there."

The line was quiet for several seconds.

"Zane?"

"Yeah?"

"If she comes out here, I mean, this is hard to say, but she can't stay with me. My boyfriend, well, it's not a good time for him and—"

Emmaline had changed her tune from their earlier conversation and Zane couldn't hide his impatience.

"So, you're going to turn my sister away? That's what you're telling me?"

"Look, Zane, it's not that I don't want to help but it sounds like she's in a lot of trouble and we can't bring that kind of thing here."

"I can't believe you, Em. I can't believe you're saying this."

More silence then a tiny *I'm sorry* from the woman he once thought he loved and that Lettie looked up to like a big sister.

"Just call me if you hear from her," Zane said.

In one smooth move he swiped the call to an end and opened the Instagram app on his phone where he had left it last: Emmaline's profile. The latest gauzy selfie photo showed Emmaline in sports bra and black tights, a pink boxing glove dangling by a string from one shoulder outside some sort of exercise studio. "Never stop learning, because life never stops teaching!" read the chirpy caption. "Trying out boxing because —why not? Great way to turn strangers into friends is to slug a punching bag next to them!" Among the hashtags #livelovelife, #knockouttime and #poppedmyboxingcherry was #SponsoredContent. Zane couldn't believe Emmaline had found someone to pay her for her social media posts. Los Angeles truly was a city of dreams if you could get paid for stupid slogans and selfies.

He flung the phone across the bed in disgust. Good luck

with your new boxing friends, because you're certainly losing your old ones.

The airport on a Saturday morning bustled with people, all seeming to be focused exclusively on luggage and destinations. An older white man, wearing a blue airport vest, stood at a desk helpfully marked Airport Information. He smiled at Zane and Angel and they made their way to him.

"I wonder if you've seen my sister. She's missing and we think she may have come to the airport."

Zane held out his phone to show the man a selfie Lettie had posted online a few days ago.

The man peered at the phone through his reading glasses for what seemed like forever.

"A lot of people come through here," he said. "Not everyone stops by here. Where do you think she's going?"

"Los Angeles."

"If I were you, I'd try Southwest then. They've got the cheapest tickets and the most flights." He pointed to the ticket counter to the right, where about ten people waited in line.

Angel and Zane moved along with the small wave of people heading for the ticket counter. They finally reached the ticket counter after ten excruciatingly long minutes. Zane's stomach was growling from hunger, and they got the same blank look and negative response from the ticket agent, a red-haired woman with a sharp nose.

She handed back the phone then held up a finger.

"Marlene, come here a sec," she said, gesturing toward another ticket agent about ten feet away.

"Weren't you telling me you had someone pay you cash today for a ticket? Like, actual dollars?"

A woman of about sixty in a starched blue shirt nodded and

stepped closer to the other agent, leaving the family she had been waiting on to continue scribbling out their addresses onto tiny paper luggage tags.

"Yup," Marlene said. "Why?" She looked more interested than she should have been, Zane thought. One of those gossipy types all too willing to nose into other people's business. However much he hated the tendency, he was smart enough to seize the opportunity to get some information on his sister.

"This guy here is looking for his little sister. She's run away."

Zane showed her a photo of Lettie, her tongue out and her head crooked to one side.

"Oh yeah, I remember her," the woman said. "She wasn't the one that paid all cash though. She had a credit card."

Of course she did, Zane thought. Probably a stolen one.

Marlene moved back to the family waiting for her to check them in. The mother cleared her throat emphatically. She wasn't someone who looked like she liked waiting on people to help her.

"Getting a cold?" Marlene said to the woman who offered up a closed-lip smile that had no joy in it.

"Where did she want to go to?"

"Los Angeles," Marlene said, fingers tapping out a staccato rhythm on a hidden keyboard. "She should be landing there in about two hours."

"How much is a ticket on the next flight?" Zane asked.

The next flight left in five hours and cost five hundred dollars. Zane pulled out his credit card and bought the ticket, knowing he was spending money he didn't really have, but for him, there was no choice. He'd have to go to the zoo and plead with Gerry to keep the job open for him while he went to L.A.

"Maybe I can help you out with the money," Angel said.

"Isn't that the kind of thing that got us into this mess?"

"I have my own money." His mouth drooped. "I want to come with you at least."

"No way. I can't take care of you in L.A."

"I'll be safer with you anyway."

Angel had a point, Zane thought, but he couldn't afford two plane tickets. He was already going to be paying this charge off for months. Plus, how was he going to get around L.A.? He'd have to rent a car too, and that was probably going to be another five hundred. Emmaline had made it clear he couldn't count on her for much. He never thought she'd be one of those people who got a taste of success and then turned her back on her friends, but sure enough, that was what Hollywood had done to her. He should have guessed it from her relentlessly boasting posts since she'd moved to L.A., selfies at the entrances to movie studios and from fancy houses with lush gardens over-looking scrubby, dry hills, a view of the Hollywood sign. To Zane it had felt like she gained entrance to a society where money flowed and good times were easy to come by, but he had taken heart in thinking that she hadn't changed that much. If he were honest, he should have known better. He had always viewed Emmaline through a fog of attraction (love, he had thought) but she'd always put herself first and foremost.

The ticket agent handed Zane the ticket. "You need to be at the gate forty-five minutes before the flight departure," she said. "There's no assigned seating so you line up by these numbers at the top."

"I've never flown anywhere before," Zane said.

"It's kind of like riding the bus, but up high," Angel said. "And faster."

"I hope you find your sister," the agent said.

They left without Angel making any more comments about buying a ticket, so Zane figured he had dropped the idea.

From the car Zane listened to the long voicemail from

Maxine. The pentagram under Lettie's bed was simply her sacred space, a place to work magic, Maxine said. She couldn't know much more about what Lettie was trying to do without more information. But it could be possible that Lettie was trying a banishing spell. Zane hung up the voicemail without feeling like he knew any more than before he listened.

"Want to see where I work?" Angel's face transformed from worried to childlike enthusiasm in seconds. Zane wished he felt the same joy at the prospect of the zoo, but the conversation with Gerry was going to be anything but fun.

Chapter Eighteen

The zoo on this good weather Saturday morning was a cheerful place. Even full of anxiety, Zane felt a mood boost from the friendly buzz emanating off the family ahead, a red balloon sailing behind the smallest child, a lion's face printed on it, tied around her wrist by a blue ribbon. They were on the path to the giraffe barn, the smell of popcorn mixing with the slightly sour, earthy smell of the animals. Angel's excitement almost matched the kids'.

"I haven't been here since I was five or six" he said. "Can we go see the lions?"

Under the brilliance of a late morning sun, the crowd was relaxed, stopping and starting and changing directions, consulting maps, taking photos. Pigeons beaked at dropped popcorn kernels. One of the zookeepers stood in the center of a group of kids, a fuzzy lemur looping its way from her left shoulder to her right, then placing its paw on her head. Angel paused, aimed his phone at her.

"It's just like the opening of Zoo Tycoon," Angel said.

"When the game starts there's always a zookeeper holding a lemur."

"You need to spend more time in the real world," Zane said. He felt on edge, his nerves jangling with worry about Lettie and this unshakeable fear of hurtling through the air in a long metal tube for five hours.

The zookeeper with the lemur guided the animal back to her shoulder with a small treat she pulled out of the fanny pack around her waist. "The word lemur is Latin. It means spirits of the night," she said. "Some people think they're supernatural beings, like ghosts. But I think that was mainly because they are most active at night."

An electric golf cart hummed behind them. "You're early today," Gerry said, wedged behind the steering wheel and peering at him from behind dark aviator glasses. The cart's steering wheel pressed into his thick belly. It didn't look comfortable.

Not watching where he was going, Zane stumbled over a rock and fell to the ground. The bricks of the walkway scraped his palms. Particles of dirt dug into his skin and the lower part of his right hand was cut and bled.

He stood up, brushing his hands off, embarrassed.

"You all right there, buddy?" Gerry held out a bottle of water, gesturing as if he would pour it over Zane's hands. Zane waved him off and wiped his hands on his jeans instead. His palms stung.

"My sister's missing," Zane said. "She's run away and I need to go get her."

"You got a shift starting in an hour," Gerry said.

"I'm going to miss it, and tomorrow," Zane said.

Gerry started breathing through his mouth, exposing a row of yellowed teeth under his sea lion whiskers.

"That's a tough one," he said. "We need you to work those shifts."

"I gotta do this," Zane said.

"I get it," Gerry said. "But I got to take action too. I'm gonna have to find someone else to cover and it might be permanent."

Zane had thought Gerry would give him a hard time about the time off but he didn't think he would take it this far.

"I'd appreciate it if you could hold the job for me. I really need it." It was as close to begging as Zane wanted to come.

"I gotta do what I gotta do, just like you," Gerry said.

Chapter Nineteen

Zane asked Angel to drive him to the airport. He had no idea how long he would be there and he didn't want to pay for parking. But instead of pulling up to wide glass doors leading to the ticketing area, Angel turned left into the long-term parking lot and took a ticket at the rickety gate.

"I'm coming with you. I bought my ticket online," he said. "And I've got money. I can help out with the expenses."

Zane thought of something his sponsor said about letting the universe do its work on you. Something about letting things fall into place, allowing a natural order to occur. Not to try to bend situations to your will. He didn't want to take any money from Angel. He trusted the kid after seeing his affection for Lettie, but a sliver of doubt remained. He would have to stay watchful.

But the truth was he could use money and he probably could use the help, and Lettie was more likely to listen to Angel than to him. So he resigned himself to his new travel companion.

"Sorry you lost your job," Angel said.

This reminded Zane he still needed to call Bingo Pratt and tell him he wouldn't be there tonight or tomorrow. He took the chicken's way out, texting Bingo that he was heading to L.A. to find his sister and didn't know when he'd be back. He didn't have the energy for another conversation about it.

The line for security had grown since they were there in the morning. "You've got to take off your shoes and put them through the X-ray," Angel said. A guy in a grey uniform shirt said the same thing, adding a part about taking large electronics out too.

"See this security checkpoint? That's kind of like the work me and Lettie did for Gene and the others. We were the frontline. We took these long lists of—," Angel paused to look around to see if anyone was paying attention to what he said. "We took these long lists of *numbers* and would make these small transactions with them. Testing them, you know, to see if they worked."

Zane wasn't sure the metaphor worked for Angel, but he wanted to know more about how the credit card ring functioned.

"Yeah, you mentioned that at the strip club. Setting up fake accounts on websites and buying stuff. What I'm curious about is how do they get the numbers?"

"A type of hacking called SQL injection."

"Sequel injection?"

"It's an acronym for something. I don't remember what. S.Q.L. Basically it's a computer programming language."

The man they met at the strip club didn't seem like the sort of nerd who'd know anything about SQL injection. He seemed more like the fists and weapons and threats type. Wally Zittman didn't seem like the tech brains either. "Who does that stuff?"

"I don't know. Most of the operation had to do with selling the stuff. All kinds of numbers, if you know what I mean."

Zane reached the security line conveyor belt, removing his sneakers and dumping his keys, phone and wallet into small round plastic bowl. He felt strange, standing there in socks, worried the phone wouldn't work after passing through the machine. No one else seemed concerned.

The plane was boarding as they arrived at the gate. Zane hadn't realized how close they cut it. The flight attendant told them they could sit toward the back if they wanted window seats and Zane bumped his way down the narrow aisle to the back with the duffle bag containing his clothes. Angel hadn't been kidding. It was like a bus. Except the Greyhound bus they'd taken a few times to MacAlester to visit Lettie's dad in prison had bigger seats.

Angel insisted he take the window seat, so he buckled in with the duffle bag stowed at his feet. Zane stared out the window at the man throwing luggage onto a conveyor belt and into the cargo hold. The plane felt claustrophobic, the air too dry, the light too bright. To take his mind off of the nips of uneasiness building inside, he resumed their conversation from the security line.

"So you said something about numbers, all kinds of numbers?"

"Right, yeah. Not just credit card numbers. Social security numbers, tax ID numbers, basically whatever you need for identity theft," Angel said in a low voice. "On the Internet, we're just a bunch of numbers in a database really. It's just not that hard to recreate."

"But it is against the law."

"Yeah."

A woman's voice over the loudspeaker asked for their attention. Zane pulled out the safety card in the seat pocket in front of him, just like she asked.

"No one really pays attention to that," Angel said.

"Yeah, well, I've never done this before." Zane watched as the flight attendant demonstrating the safety checks fastened and unfastened a seatbelt loop in the air. He checked his own seatbelt—he'd managed that much all right. Now he looked for the nearest emergency exit, which was behind him, near the bathrooms. When the woman's voice got to the part about putting on your own oxygen mask before helping others, a thought came to him. He should have called Old Spice to tell him he was going to Los Angeles. Just as an insurance policy. He resolved to call when he landed.

Angel seemed to read Zane's attention to the safety measures as worry about the flight. "You know, thousands of flights take off and land every day, all without crashing. Nothing to worry about."

"It's not like there's anything you can do save yourself if this thing goes down," Zane said. "We're pretty much in the pilot's hands."

"That's true," Angel said. He had pulled one of those hand-held video game consoles out of his backpack and stared at the main menu, a white box lined with squares of colorful game titles. His gaze rested on it for a few seconds then he set it down.

"There's this whole part of the ring now that is moving into health insurance fraud too," Angel said. "People pay for information about other people's medical records or go and get medical care under someone else's name through their insurance."

"They do all through that SQL thing you were talking about?"

"Some of it is mail theft too. They've got some contact

working at that trash sorting place, you know, where the recycling goes after it has been dumped. They collect documents people throw away, use that to recreate identities."

"How much money are you talking about?"

"It has got to be a lot, but I don't know."

"How much were they paying you and Lettie?"

"A couple hundred dollars a week."

"That doesn't seem like much," Zane said. It irritated him. Lettie could have made that much working at that carnival or another type of legal job.

"Yeah, but it was only like a few hours of work," Angel said. "And we could have made more. They were always looking for people to work on their social accounts. They have all these accounts where they try to rip people off—fake Instagram and Facebook accounts selling rare dog breeds or hard-to-get sneakers. There's all this digital housekeeping that goes with that."

Zane didn't know how to feel about hearing that Angel and his sister were apparently too lazy to make more money helping thieves steal stuff.

"You spend the first twenty minutes or so just getting set up on the RDP." Angel paused. "That stands for remote desktop protocol. Basically it is a way to connect to other people's computers, so it looks like you're using their computer and not your own."

"Jeez," Zane said. It was actually kind of impressive. Maybe Lettie could get a job in IT or something after all this. When she was home safely. When this was over.

As the plane climbed higher, Zane saw spread out below him grids of crackerbox homes and bright and tender green treetops in the bright afternoon sun. Farther out the houses gave way to fields glowing with new growth in tidy rows, a farmer on a tractor in one of them, chugging slowly. He felt something he hadn't expected to feel until he got Lettie home safely: a sense of relief. He knew it was temporary but in this moment, on this steel tube climbing through the air, time was suspended. There was nothing more he could do. Everything was out of his hands.

He bent forward, gazing out the window: creamy clouds, the sky as blue as heaven, the new green of the fields. From up here it all appeared miraculous, dazzling. He remembered Ernest telling him about his connection to the earth, and strangely, being thousands of feet above the planet made the connection stronger. What was the old saying about only knowing how much you love something when you lose it? The heavy responsibility of caring for his sister was not a tether. It was the stuff of the life, the way plants grow roots and connect the soil with the sky. He had to make her safe again. His fear for her in this big city cut like a razor across skin. It didn't matter what she was involved in, or what it took to get her out of it. He would follow her into danger as many times as he had to.

Chapter Twenty

The text message from Emmaline must have come during the long flight.

She's here with me.

Relief flooded through him. He quickly put Emmaline's address into the navigation app on his phone. The place where she lived was called North Hollywood, and the app estimated it would take Zane about an hour and twenty minutes to drive the twenty-two miles there from the airport. That was bad traffic, he thought. In Tulsa, you could usually equate the number of miles with the number of minutes driving time. Twenty-two miles roughly equaled twenty-two minutes, give or take.

Driving a rental car northeast on an hour and a half of freeways, among more cars than Zane had ever seen moving together across six lanes of traffic, landed them on a narrow, congested street. Zane maneuvered the car into a tight space in front of a two-story stucco apartment building plastered with handmade signs demanding owners "curb their dogs." The signs were useless, Zane thought, picking his way through a minefield of dog poop on the strips of grass next to sidewalk.

A bank of massive five-story apartment buildings cast a deep shadow on this smaller, rundown building. The wind flapped a sign on one of the big buildings reading "NoHo Arts District," suggesting a neighborhood on the upswing. Zane wondered if he had written Emmaline's address down wrong. Surely she lived in one of these modern buildings boasting in-unit washers and dryers, granite countertops, and free wifi. If he were honest, he'd imagined her in more a sparkling, pretty neighborhood, one like you might see on television, with wide streets and green lawns, palm trees lining the avenues. This neighborhood had a slightly more tumbledown feel.

The metal security door was propped open with a brick. Zane pulled it open and entered the apartment's courtyard. Television laugh tracks and the smell of broiling meat wafted out of screen doors open in the afternoon heat. An acid-green pool surrounded by sunburned shrubs glittered in the sun.

Emmaline Perryman looked beautiful, gossamer-thin and pale, clad in leggings and a tank-top suggesting she'd just finished a workout. The perfectly winged eyeliner and layers of necklaces and bracelets suggested otherwise. He moved toward her for a hug but she shrank back and awkwardly stuck out her hand to him as though they were strangers.

She had bleached her hair. It surprised him. Her brown hair had gone golden and had the effect of setting off her eyes, intensifying her gaze. Was this the hair color Emmaline thought she had to have to make it in reality television?

"It's good to see you," she said. A nervous glance over her shoulder toward a shadowy figure standing behind a metal screen door.

"So nice to see you once again, Ms. Perryman," Zane said, shaking her slightly damp hand. He didn't want to let her oddness go unremarked.

"Where is she?" he said.

"She took off when she heard you were coming," Emmaline said. Her words stung like angry hornets. Could it also be that Emmaline chased Lettie away because of that boyfriend she mentioned?

"You must be Angel," she said, shaking his hand too. "Lettie couldn't stop talking about you. Come inside for a moment and I'll tell you what happened."

She pulled the screen door open and ushered them inside. The apartment was tinier than Zane had been expecting. Tinier even then his place in Tulsa. Certainly tinier than the mobile home where Emmaline's parents lived, where she grew up. Of course he knew everyone embellished their success on the Internet, but he hadn't imagined such a stark contrast for Emmaline.

The apartment smelled like marijuana smoke. Out of the dim light emerged a slick-haired man with arms covered in thick black tribal tattoos. He had short legs and too much muscle, reminding Zane of a bulldog. Before he could stop the thought, he had imagined them in bed, this sinewy man absorbing her, grunting and drooling.

"You must be Zane," the bulldog man said. "I'm Colt."

The guy who Zane assumed basically chased his sister out into the L.A. streets grinned at him like he was king of the castle. Zane wanted to punch him. Instead he shook his hand for the benefit of the audience of Angel and Emmaline. Bulldog man's hand was cold and damp from the beer he now gripped in his left.

"Tough news about your sister," he said.

Zane tried to keep the anger out of his voice. Emmaline's words rang in his head: *it's not that I don't want to help but it sounds like she's in a lot of trouble and we can't bring that kind of thing here.* "I wish you all could have kept her here," he said. "Lettie thinks of Emmaline as her big sister."

"Is that right?" Colt took a swig of the beer and plopped down in a brown velour recliner to regard Zane. A nasty looking knife with a viciously sharp blade laid on its side on the coffee table, casual as a drink coaster or a magazine next to a rolling tray, papers and small bag of marijuana. Bulldog man rested the beer on his thigh, which bobbed up and down like an oil jack. "You didn't tell me that, Emmaline."

Emmaline shrugged. "I said we all grew up together in Tulsa," she said. She went to sit on the arm of the recliner and wiped some invisible piece of lint off of his cheek. She slurred the word Tulsa a little at the end and Zane realized she was stoned. They both were.

"So how did she get here? Did someone drive her?"

"No idea," Emmaline said. "She didn't say. You know, there's a subway just two blocks away. She could have taken that."

"That subway don't go to the airport, Em. You know that. Stupid city planners built the subway but stopped short of the airport. Stupid, huh?"

"Yeah, but you can get there with that bus service," she said meekly.

"Bottom line is we don't know how she got here," Colt said.

"She called me when she was outside the building," Emmaline said. "I told her you were coming out and she should stick around. She acted like she would, but basically she just came in, used the bathroom, took a bottle of water and left again."

"Where does that subway go?"

"All over," Emmaline said. "Hollywood, downtown, Long Beach, Santa Monica."

"I thought we were in Hollywood," Angel said.

This drew a snort from Colt. "This is *North* Hollywood. Wrong side of the Hollywood Hills. Welcome to the San

Fernando Valley, buddy. The suburbs, basically, and yes, home to the porn industry."

"That's not true, Colt," Emmaline said. "The porn studios are all way out north in Chatsworth. And there's plenty of real studios out here. Disney and Warner Brothers are just down the road in Burbank."

Colt's face collapsed into a mean smirk. "I'll just ignore the fact that my girlfriend knows exactly where the porn studios are."

Emmaline stood up and grabbed the remote control from the coffee table, drawing Zane's attention once again to the knife. It had a handle that looked like antler horn. It looked heavy and primitive, not like something you bought at the sporting goods store.

"She can't stand that commercial about the abused dogs," Colt said. "Turns the channel every time."

"Yeah, Lettie hates that one too, and the one with the cancer kids," Angel said.

The air conditioning was on much too high in the apartment and Zane felt like he was inhaling refrigerant. He told himself what he always told himself when confronted with Emmaline and her problematic choices in men: *It's not my business.*

"Did Lettie give any clue where she was going?" he asked. He wondered if Lettie had partaken in the marijuana with them. If she was wandering around North Hollywood stoned and scared. Or worse, stoned and too trusting.

Colt wasn't looking at Zane, but at Emmaline as she scrolled through the television channel guide. Framed photos of some of Emmaline's old pageant gown customers hung on the wall to the right of the television. "She asked me if I knew if there was any kind of occult store around here," Emmaline said.

"Is there?"

"What do you think?" Colt smirked. "It's La La Land. Of course there is."

On the television, a group of kids made cookies for some kind of baking competition show. "There are so many more cooking competition shows than sewing ones," Emmaline said. "Maybe I should learn how to bake."

"I thought you were in the running for a new show," Zane said.

Colt turned his dulled eyes toward Zane. "She wishes," he said. "She couldn't even land a waitressing job this week."

Emmaline flushed bright red. "I've gotten a few callbacks," she said. "It's a tough business. No one is an overnight sensation."

Disgust thundered through him. She was lying to everyone, including herself. She lived in a fantasy world and he had real world problems. He didn't have any more time for Emmaline.

"So where's the occult store?" he blurted out.

"The Bloodrose. It's just down Lankershim." Emmaline pointed toward the door. "That way about five or six blocks I think. Maybe ten."

Zane managed a thanks, pushing past his irritation at the time wasted. Lettie could have already been to the Bloodrose and gone by the time these two potheads got the information out. He nodded to Angel, and they walked to the door, past a white and grey cat licking its paws. It looked up at them as they left.

Outside, the sun warmed Zane's hands and face. He had wanted to believe in Emmaline's success. Had even felt intimidated by it. He wanted to be angry with her, for not helping him and Lettie, for lying to him. For years of selfish behavior. But seeing the reality had only made him sad.

"She wasn't what I expected," Angel said.

"Nope, she sure has changed." Away from Emmaline, his disgust morphed into a wave of pity for her and her warped life. She'd lost everything real about her to this façade she had created. He'd seen all he needed to see from her.

Chapter Twenty-One

Still cold from the apartment, Zane shut off the rental car's air conditioning and rolled down the windows as he drove down a wide street lined with RVs, campers and a few tents. Urban camping, a clear sign that Los Angeles had a serious problem with homelessness. If Lettie had walked the mile's distance to the Bloodrose, had she taken this street? Would anyone have tried to bother her? The area seemed fraught with danger to him: big urban streets with cars whizzing past and only a handful of people walking, heads down, looking at their phones. If Lettie had struggled with anyone, no one would have noticed.

The Bloodrose was located on a busy street between a tile store and a place advertising faxes and printers on an enormous blue billboard attached the front. It was a two-story cottage, covered in olive-green stucco with a grid of thick dark wood beams surrounding four small opaque windows. A small, hand-lettered sign hung to the left of a thick wooden door studded with metal nails. On a street of uniform storefronts, the store stood out like the witch's cottage in the Hansel and Gretel fairy tale, minus the candy.

The store was small. As they walked inside, a man behind the counter called out "Welcome," then continued to work with the only other customer there. The man was grinding something in a huge stone mortar and pestle on the green counter. Behind him was a massive carved wooden bookshelf lined with glass jars filled with what looked like spices in every color of the rainbow. There was an arrow-shaped wooden sign reading "Psychics and Healers" that pointed to the back of the store. The store smelled earthy, a blend of lavender and patchouli and cardamom. "We can hand pour a candle for you too," the man said, sliding what looked like a menu to the customer in front of him.

Like Earth Spells, the displays in the store featured a lot of amulets, statues, jewelry and stones. In the glass case nearest the door, a dozen or so highly carved wands sat nestled on purple velvet. Zane chalked up the difference between the two to the Hollywood influence: where Earth Spells felt like a generic store filled with psychic objects and books, The Blood-rose felt like a *Harry Potter* movie set depicting the school of magic. Or the school of magic's old-fashioned apothecary. The vibe, from the thick green carpet to the plant vines dripping off of exposed wooden beams to the artful display of the objects, was distinctly fantasy. He wouldn't have been surprised to see the proprietor dressed in magical robes embroidered with stars and moons.

Zane picked up a laminated booklet on top of the case entitled "Magical Advice and Custom Spellcrafting" and paged through it. It seemed to have a spell for just about any problem.

Protection Spell Kit to be used at the new moon. Healing Spell Kit, to heal your body, your psyche or your life. It is useful when you are ill or have parted from a loved one. A Spell for Wealth. A Spell for Companionship.

Zane turned to find a young woman standing behind him. She had tattooed arms and wore a flowy dress with tall cowboy boots, a similar bohemian outfit vibe as Maxine had worn in Tulsa. Some things were the same everywhere. She rat-a-tatted long blue fingernails on the wand case. "Beautiful, aren't they?" She gestured to the wands.

"Yeah," Zane said.

"In the market or just looking around?"

"We're looking for someone," Angel said. "Someone who may have come in here today."

"My sister," Zane said. He pulled out the phone and showed the woman a photo of Lettie.

She studied the photo for a long moment, rocking back and forth on the heels of her boots. Her skirt swayed over bare tan legs.

"Is she in some kind of trouble?"

"Yes," Zane said. "Bad people are looking for her."

The woman handed the phone back then twisted a lock of hair nervously. "How do I know you're not the bad people?" she said.

"I'm Zane Clearwater. Lettie is my youngest sister. This here is Angel, her boyfriend. We flew all the way out here from Oklahoma a few hours ago to find her and bring her home. We're pretty sure she came here. If there's anything you can tell us about her or where she may have gone, we'd appreciate it."

The woman looked them over as though taking their measure.

"We're the ones who care about her the most," Angel said. "Her mom died in a fire not too long ago. Her dad's in prison. She ran away from her grandma's house because she was scared people were coming to get here. We're trying to keep her safe."

She straightened some beaded bracelets on a hanging display that didn't need straightening.

"She was in here," she said. "She seemed nervous. She wanted to buy some stuff for spells."

"Protection spells?" Angel asked.

"Banishing your enemy type of spells," the woman said. "Protection too. She talked to John more than me. He's the co-owner."

Zane glanced back at the man at the counter, who was now scooping the contents of the pestle into a paper bag.

"Do you know where she went after she left?"

The woman shook her head. "She didn't say anything to me."

The other customer's departure made a small bell hanging from the door clang. John came around the counter to them. He was a white guy with a narrow nose and high cheekbones, somewhere in his fifties. Tall and rail-thin, he was wearing a green T-shirt, jeans and old Doc Martens. His gray hair was cropped close, revealing the dents and irregularities of his skull. His fingers were covered in silver rings, a skull, a wolf's head, an Egyptian ankh. Around his neck was a shark's-tooth pendant hanging from a thick leather cord.

"I'm John," he said warmly. "Is there something I can help you with?"

"My sister was in here a little while ago," Zane said. The woman chimed in, recounting the story they'd just told her like a detective might brief his boss on a new case. Angel flashed his phone at the man with what Zane assumed was a photo of Lettie.

John inspected the photo for another minute, eyes narrowed. Then he ran his eyes over Zane and Angel.

"You look worried," he said. "She looked worried too."

"Do you know where she went?"

John blinked and Zane had the sense the man was holding back still, waiting to come to some decision about him and Angel. Maybe trying to read their aura or something. Normally Zane would have lost patience with this kind of hesitation. But there was something about John that gave him hope that the man would help. His gaze was direct and searching, he looked like Dumbledore's new age younger brother, and he spoke in a minister's comforting tone.

"We've come a long way to find her," Angel said.

"The thing is, when someone comes in for a protection spell—and more—and then in come two people trying to find that person—," John said. And then he shook his head. "One has to pause and try to understand what is going on."

"We're trying to help her," Zane said. "But bad people are after her. She stole something from them."

"People come to Los Angeles to escape all sorts of things," John said. He rolled the shark's tooth pendant thoughtfully between his fingers.

"She's fifteen."

"Being young doesn't necessarily mean she doesn't have good judgment," John said. "She told me she had hoped to stay with a friend here but that friend let her down."

"Yeah, that's where we just came from," Zane said. "Look, I don't know how to prove to you that I'm trying to help her, not hurt her. I don't know how you can know what's in someone's heart when you meet them for five minutes. But I don't have a lot of time to stand here and try to convince you of anything. My sister's somewhere in this city with bad people after her and I want to get her home. She's all I have."

John stared at Zane for a moment before answering, his face unreadable.

"Just wait here for a few minutes," he said. With that, he pivoted toward the back and disappeared down a long hallway, toward the "Psychics and Healers" area. Zane wondered if he was going to have his tarot cards read or something. These occult people could sometimes go sideways on you.

The brass bell on the door chimed as another customer entered, this time a young man with the orange glow of a spray-tan addict, probably an actor trying to make it in the same scene Emmaline was. He stopped at a display of books near the front and picked up one called *Drawing Money*. Good luck with that, Zane thought. His mother had spent plenty of money on candles and such to bring money to the family, but it seemed like the money only flowed out.

"I'll be right back," the woman said. "My name is Tamara by the way."

Zane went to the counter to peer at the shelves stocked with herbs and oils. Row upon row of glass jars, some clear and unlabeled, revealing dries flowers, berries, leaves, and even a few that looked like plain brown dirt. To the left were smaller dark bottles with green labels, reading: Hawthorn Berry, High John the Conqueror Root, Abramelin, Bat's Blood. For all he knew, it was real bat's blood in the bottle.

"I know Lettie's into this but I don't really get it," Angel said in a low voice. "Don't people see that it's just wishful thinking?" He held up a bottle from a smaller display on the counter. "This oil says it will help attract a wealthy partner. A series of seduction and commitment herbs."

"Obviously Lettie didn't use that to hook you," Zane joked.

Angel smiled. "If only they had one of these to get me a sponsorship deal for my YouTube channel," he said.

"Look around, I'm sure it's here," Zane said.

Another ten minutes passed before John re-entered the room, calm as a monk with his hands folded in front of his chest. "Sorry for the delay," he said. "I had to spend some time meditating on what to do."

"And what did you decide?"

"I decided to help you out." John held out a bright green sticky note to Zane with some writing on it.

"This is the place I told your sister about," he said. "It's a place for homeless youth in Hollywood. I told her how to get there on the subway. She said she needed a place to stay and it had to be cheap."

A new arrow of worry hit Zane. Had she run out of money just getting to L.A.? He realized he had been hoping that she had one of those stolen credit cards, even though he disapproved of the use. He preferred thinking about her safe in a motel room somewhere rather than wandering Hollywood looking for a free place to stay.

"She's trying to hide," Angel said. "It's like she's waiting for something to pass."

"Or to happen," Zane said. "Would she be trying to sell that information she took from those guys?"

"She doesn't know anyone else in L.A.," Angel said. "Other than Emmaline."

"So what does she want with that info?"

"It's either leverage to keep herself safe or—" Angel stopped. "Like you said, she's trying to sell it."

"How would she do that, in a city where she knows no one?"

"The same way she'd do it in Tulsa," Angel said. "On the dark web."

Chapter Twenty-Two

Zane insisted on stopping by the North Hollywood police station to report Lettie missing. Angel thought it felt like a waste of time. Zane didn't want to tell him the real reason: that he was fearful if something bad happened to Lettie that he'd never know.

The officer who took the report had a lot of questions, asked with a brisk kindness that suggested she had filled out many of these forms before and not had a lot of success seeing any good come from them. Besides the height, weight, hair color questions Zane had expected, she also asked about tattoos, whether she smoked or drank, what kind of places she liked to go to, what she was wearing, psychological problems, whether or not she knew how to drive.

The officer, whose nametag read R. Lopez, had brought them to a small interrogation room. Her questions felt like an interrogation of Zane's guardian skills. How well did he know Lettie? How well was he really looking after her? He tried to silence the critical voices in his head and reminded himself the officer was just going through a questionnaire.

"What was going on in her life the day she left? Any fights or conflicts?" Officer Lopez had long eyelashes framing slightly protruding eyes.

Angel leaned back in the plastic chair, as though to distance himself from the question. Zane wondered, and not for the first time, who had gotten who mixed up in this ring.

"She got involved with some bad people," Zane said. "Back in Tulsa." He walked her through Wally Zittman's death, Perrine's visit to the apartment, the trip to their grandmother's house and Lettie's departure. He held back the information that she'd taken some property from the men who sought her. He understood the importance, but didn't want to implicate Lettie in the crimes any more than he had to.

"Do the Tulsa Police know she's missing?"

Zane's mind flashed with images of the night at Bamboozles, the smell of tires burning as Perrine made his getaway. He'd held back from Old Spice too, telling him Lettie was missing but leaving out his sister's poorly thought-out blackmail plan or whatever it was from the detective for the same reasons he did so with Officer Lopez. He wanted the police's help in finding Lettie, but he didn't want to make things worse than they had to be. That's why he wanted to be the one to find her. He would set things right. That was his job as her big brother and her guardian.

Zane nodded and pulled out his phone so he could give the officer Old Spice's phone number, impatient to get this over with and drive over to the shelter in Hollywood.

"Is there anything else we should know? About her health? Does she take any medications like insulin or anything else?"

Angel leaned forward in the chair. It was obvious to Zane that he wanted to say something and Zane was afraid he was going to blurt out Lettie's blackmail plan. He shot the teen a look that said keep it quiet.

Angel opened his mouth and then shut it again. Officer Lopez was enough of a trained observer to catch their interaction and paused, eyes fixed on Angel.

"Is there something you want to tell me?"

"I don't know," Angel said.

"Do you want to talk privately?" Officer Lopez asked.

Angel white-knuckled the edge of the table for a moment, as though bracing himself for one of California's earthquakes.

"It's just—she's pregnant," Angel said.

Chapter Twenty-Three

"You were going to tell me when exactly?" Zane said to Angel as they left the police station. A police car pulled into the parking lot, flashing lights streaking the air.

"I thought it was something Lettie and I should tell you together." Angel, who had been checking his phone, glanced up at Zane with an innocent expression.

"Ideally, sure," muttered Zane. He gave Angel a sharp look. "How far along is she?"

"We think it's two months. She was going to go to the doctor to get checked out but then all this happened."

"Have you two talked about what you're going to do?"

Angel looked like a lost little kid, standing there next to the North Hollywood Police Station sign as though he wanted to go back inside. People talk about a sinking feeling in their stomachs when they got news like this. Zane felt like his whole body was sinking, a sensation so persistent he wouldn't have been surprised if an earthquake opened a chasm in front of him.

"She wants to keep the baby. I do too."

"You are kids yourself," Zane said.

"We love each other."

"It takes more than love to make things like this work." Zane's anger and anxiety grew, permeating the air between them, creating a forcefield of energy around them that caused a couple leaving the station to take a wide berth around them. He was flooded with images of Lettie. As a toddler, she had waddled after him everywhere like a puppy dog. In second grade, she'd asked if she could bring him to class for parents' day. Her pride at winning some essay contest about citizenship in fifth grade. Through it all, even when he was at his worst, fighting and drinking, he'd always seen Lettie as a basket of hope. The one member of their little family with the brightest trajectory. Now that had changed again, this time more permanently.

"We're going to make it work," Angel said. "You'll see."

"I hope so." Zane could tell from Angel's earnest expression that he really meant it, but anguish spread through him like a thick rust, consuming the last bits of hope he held to get on her a traditional path of high school to college to good-paying job. He hadn't realized how big his dreams for her had been, or how this news changed his own expectations. If Lettie, his smarter, sweeter sister, couldn't break out of the narrow straits of their life at the bottom of economic food chain, how was it not his fault?

The parking lot at My Friend's Place was cracked and weedy and surrounded by a bent chain-link fence. Trash and dry weeds hugged the fence line. The sky above them was a thick white cloud cover, solid as milk. The Hollywood Freeway they had just exited ran below them just steps away in a deep channel. Cement K-rails were all that kept cars or people from tumbling down the slope to the cars below.

It was a depressing place. A lone palm tree emerged from the slope, its trunk covered in shaggy dead fronds. It looked like a shabby, thick imposter of the iconic swaying palms that decorated Hollywood postcards. So far, Los Angeles was not impressive.

The weather had grown cooler as the day progressed and Zane zipped up his hoodie. Another myth: sunny Los Angeles was not so sunny either.

Still, as he got out of the rental car, a feeling of hope swept through him like a memory of a happy dream. Maybe they would find Lettie inside. He took a deep breath, but by the time he had exhaled, the hope was gone again and the spring wind made the ugly palm tree flutter its fronds. Hollywood on a Saturday afternoon, single drivers alone in their cars, running the last of their errands before the evening set in, the steady buzz of the freeway below and pigeons circling and landing. How wonderful that would be, to be concerned with grocery lists or dinner plans or bills instead of a missing, pregnant sister.

Zane and Angel entered the building through the entrance off the parking lot. Zane had never been in a shelter like this before and he was surprised how bright and cheerful it was. The lobby could have been mistaken for one of those start-up technology companies they showed on television, the ones with ping-pong tables and hammocks and beanbags in the common areas—at least until you noticed the iron security bars on the windows and the sign pointing to where visitors could take showers. And assuming you didn't know that the young, tattooed people moving through the hallways carrying large backpacks were living on the streets.

Zane introduced himself at the reception desk to a woman with a forceful presence. Gleaming blue hair pulled back in a twisting braid, pale, crescent forehead, a curious and friendly expression emanating from her thick-lashed eyes.

"Hi there," she said. "Can I help you?" She seemed very practiced at putting people at ease.

"We're looking for my sister," Zane said. "Someone told us she came here."

The slight narrowing of the woman's eyes made Zane think he should have taken a different approach. He could feel the walls building up between them. He hadn't realized just how suspicious people became when you told them you were looking for someone who ran away. It was like they asked themselves *what did this guy do to make her want to leave?*

Zane put his hand on his chest. "I'm Zane Clearwater. This is Angel. He's my sister's boyfriend. We flew here all the way from Oklahoma today to find her. She's mixed up with some bad people and we're trying to find her and keep her safe."

The woman handed a notepad and pen to Zane in a practiced gesture. "Why don't you write a note down for her and if someone by that name comes in, I'll make sure she gets it?"

Angel held his phone out to the woman. "This is a picture of her. Has she come in?"

The woman looked at the phone for a moment but kept her facial expression neutral. "I'm not going to say," she said. "Our clients have their privacy here."

"I'm her guardian," Zane said.

"Okay, still..." she pointed to the notepad in his hand. "Let's try it my way. You write and tell her what's in your heart. If someone with that name or who looks like your sister comes in, I'll give it to her. That's the best I can do."

Zane moved to one of the red plastic chairs lining the wall to write the note. He thought of the last four text messages he had sent to her, all unanswered. He had already tried anger as well as pleading and bargaining. He couldn't even tell if she was getting them. She'd probably blocked his number.

"What do you think I should say?"

"I don't know," Angel said.

Zane sat for a moment, trying out different approaches in his head. As he sat there, he felt the room settle around him, and had a sudden odd feeling, like he felt Lettie's presence. It was as if she'd left an imprint on the air of this place, so tangible, he could almost reach out and touch her.

His whole life felt insubstantial, as if everything that mattered to him might vanish like smoke on the wind. He could not imagine the days before him if Lettie did not return safely to his care. He knew she was getting older, of course he did, and that one day she would leave, for college or her own place. But that was years off, not today, not as a fifteen-year-old girl. A pregnant fifteen-year-old *woman*, he corrected himself. A strong urge to be alone and just think for a minute struck him like a hot gust of air.

Lettie—

The building's air conditioning rumbled to life and cool air ruffled his hair. Zane turned the pen in his fingers as if the movement would help him find the words. Angel leaned his head against the painted cinderblock wall and closed his eyes. He looked like a kid, baby pudge still on his cheeks and under his chin. But his feelings ran deep for Lettie. Somehow, someway, in her first boyfriend, Lettie had managed to find someone who really cared about her. He wished he had found someone like that when he was her age. He had thought Emmaline was that person, despite tons of evidence that she wasn't. And he had relentlessly chased that dream of Emmaline for years and years, never getting closer to her heart than a friend with benefits. She didn't seem to be in a good situation with Bulldog man. But she was an adult. And she wasn't his problem. Lettie was.

The woman at the desk had gave him some advice when she handed him the notepad. *Write from your heart,* or something like that. So what was in his heart? Fear for Lettie. Fear for her safety. And now this new fear for the little life inside her. A little baby who didn't choose to be here. He would do everything he could to keep all of them—Lettie, Angel, this little baby—safe.

He pressed the pen into the paper and let the words flow.

Angel told me about the baby. Come home with me. We will figure this out together.

He signed his name and handed the notepad back to the woman at the desk without folding it over. He didn't care if she saw what he wrote.

Zane and Angel sat in the car in the parking lot of My Friend's Place. Zane couldn't shake the feeling that Lettie was inside. He went so far as to put the key in the ignition and turn the motor over, but he couldn't yet bring himself to put the car into drive and leave. She must have seen the note by now. She must be thinking about coming out now.

Angel must have felt a measure of hope too. His phone rested on his denim-clad leg face-up so he could see the screen light up with a call or text if she decided to reach out that way.

Zane ran his hands over the steering wheel feeling the fingertip grooves on the backside. Evening was only a few hours away, and it had been clear from the signs at the center that they weren't open as a place to sleep. So she'd have to come out soon. Or not. He didn't know what he would do if they didn't find Lettie today. He supposed they would need to find a place to stay in L.A. either way. In a perfect world, Emmaline would have opened up her home to all of them, but she'd made it clear her allegiances were elsewhere. She seemed scared of that boyfriend, that much was obvious. Maybe he should try to reach out to her one more time, see if he could talk some sense into her. Or maybe it was none of his business anymore. Maybe what he really needed to do was stay focused on helping Lettie.

"Tell me about the dark web," Zane said. "You mentioned that was where Lettie would try to sell whatever it is she stole."

"Basically it's the part of the web that's encrypted. You can't get there using a typical Google search or your web browser. You have to have special software and most people conceal their identities there so you don't know who you're dealing with."

The thought again crossed his mind that Lettie seemed to have quite the knack for this tech stuff. Maybe he could get her to channel that for good, for a career in computers or something. There had to be a bright lining to this.

"So people sell illegal stuff on it then? That's the purpose?"

"That's part of it but not the whole story. Some people believe that you should have the right to communicate online without the government snooping on you. And they do snoop on you, you know that?"

"You mean like reading posts on Facebook and Twitter?"

"No, I mean everything. You might think you're sending emails that only the recipient sees, but the U.S. government, if it thought you were a threat, could see them," Angel said. "Like if you were trying to protest against the government. I mean, it's your right, but do you want them watching your every electronic move all in the name of national security?"

"I don't know, I mean, they have to do things like to catch criminals, don't they?" Zane said.

"Yeah, people shouldn't break laws. But they should also have some rights, you know? The right to join organizations, and say some things anonymously and meet with people who care about the same things you do. Imagine a dictator in the

White House, using all the surveillance tools they have to track people who spoke out against him."

"Is there a way we can track Lettie's movements on the dark web?"

"No, I mean, that's precisely the point of it. Anonymity."

The shrill peal of a cell phone interrupted their conversation. Zane's eyes flew to the phone perched on Angel's leg but its screen remained black. He reached into his pocket and fished out his own phone.

It was Lettie.

Chapter Twenty-Four

The vacancy sign was lit at the Pepper Tree Lodge Motel on Lankershim, a squat, long, one-story building built like a fortress along the busy street. He circled the parking lot twice before spotting the room number Lettie had given him on the phone.

Zane's "spidey-sense" about Lettie inside My Friend's Place turned out to be all wrong. In fact, Lettie hadn't even left the North Hollywood area at all. She had left the Bloodrose and walked to the Pepper Tree Motel and booked a room for eighty dollars a night. It was one of Angel's texts that prompted her to call Zane finally. Something about the baby and his reaction to it, Zane presumed, but maybe also the idea that they might leave her here in this city alone. She didn't really say what it was specifically that made her call his number and he knew it didn't matter that much why. What mattered was that she did it.

Lettie was at the window when they walked up to the door marked 109, her face framed by the windowsill and the dingy ivory curtain she gripped in one hand. She opened the door.

"I've been so worried about you," Zane said as he threw his arms around her.

"You can see me now and I'm fine," she said, her voice muffled against his shoulder. Angel wrapped his arms around them both in a bear hug and they stood like that for a while before Lettie broke the spell.

Inside the motel room, the small television mounted on the wall blared some reality show woman driving somewhere, delivering a monologue aimed at the camera about someone named Danielle who would get what she deserved. The room was shabby and not so clean—lint had collected in patches on the flat beige carpet and hundreds of careless guests had scuffed the paint on the walls. The thin brown bedspread was wrinkled and the center of the queen-sized mattress sagged. The room smelled damp. The rumble of a truck engine outside shook the glass window.

Angel sat on the edge of the bed, bedsprings groaning like a thousand shrieking elves.

"So what do you think of Los Angeles?" Zane said, his arms still wrapped around her and his head resting on top of hers.

"I might be ready to leave," Lettie said. She pulled away from him and he felt a physical pain at their separation, like a bandage being ripped off. None of the loss in his life so far had compared with the feeling that he had lost his sister forever. He didn't want to take his eyes off of her face.

"Emmaline made it sound so good out here. All those photos she posted online. Even an hour ago, she posted this photo of her on the beach with hashtags like #bestlife and #livingthedream. I thought she lived in some awesome place and everything was going well for her. But it's all some fabrication. She lives in this dark apartment in a not very nice part of town, her boyfriend doesn't treat her right, she's stoned out of her mind, and here I am thinking she's got it made. She wouldn't even let me stay in her crappy apartment with her and that douchebag."

"I know, we were there," Zane said. "I guess I'm not surprised she'd try to put a really good front up about her life out here in La La Land."

"I'm worried about her though," Lettie said. "She doesn't have anyone out here looking out for her."

"She has Colt," Angel said, opening and closing the motel's dresser drawers as though they contained treasure.

"I think she needs someone other than Colt," Lettie said. "Maybe we should stage an intervention. She's not thinking right about that guy. He's too controlling."

Zane wasn't sure if he should be proud of Lettie for wanting to help Emmaline—and recognizing a bad relationship when she saw one—or if he should remind her just how much trouble she was in herself. He chose the latter.

"But first, tell me, what is this property you stole? Some bad people told me they're looking for you."

Angel pulled out the Bible and flipped through its pages. Prayers couldn't hurt, Zane thought.

"I do need some help," Lettie said.

"How do you mean?" Zane said. "You can tell me anything."

Lettie stared vacantly at the television screen for a moment. She sighed and gave a shrug. "Promise you won't be mad?"

Zane's anger was hot as fire, wondering what how much danger she had put herself in. Despite the overwhelming urge to take her by the shoulders and shake her, he made himself give a tight-lipped smile.

"I promise."

"See this thumb drive," Lettie said. She pulled a blue and silver rectangle out of her pants pocket and held it in the palm of her hand. Zane nodded.

"It's got a damn fortune on it."

Angel sat on the corner of the bed to a symphony of creaks. "You took the Braum's files."

Zane leaned against the edge of the dresser, feeling it shift under the pressure the way cheap furniture joints do.

"Braum's the ice cream place?" The stores dotted Tulsa streets, selling scoops of ice cream, hamburgers and shakes.

"Is it as big as they said?" Angel asked. Some kind of dark web-speak, Zane thought.

Lettie nodded. "At least ten million cards."

Angel shook his head. "Lettie," he said, "you have to give that back."

Her hand closed over the flash drive and she slipped it back in her jeans pocket.

"This is our insurance policy," she said. "This is how we're going to get out of this."

"What is this exactly?" Zane was done with feeling dumb.

"Credit card information. For ten million cards. They've been working on the Braum's slow bleed for months and months. The company doesn't even know they're skimming the card numbers. This is dangerous, Lettie."

"All that is on that little flash drive?" Zane said.

"Yes, compressed and encrypted," Lettie said. Whatever that mean, Zane thought. "Surely they have back-up," he said.

Lettie gave a maybe-maybe not smile. "They probably realized by now that their back-up is full of unicorn gifs."

"Shit, Lettie," Angel said. "I don't think those guys are going to appreciate your sense of humor there."

The conversation felt surreal. Ten million credit cards ready to be sold on the black market. The dark web, as Angel had called it. Lettie had some serious technical chops, that was for sure. But she was clearly in over her head. A hack and a theft worth a fortune, the promise of an easy life. He'd never thought of Lettie being one who would want to take shortcuts. But obviously there was a lot he didn't know about his little sister.

"Lettie, seriously, this plan of yours sounds illegal," Zane said. He tried to sound reasonable, afraid he instead would cross the line into righteous which wouldn't likely have the persuasive impact he needed.

Lettie shrugged. Angel glanced back at his phone, eyebrows raised. They had clearly already had conversations like this before, but their casualness about breaking the law was incredibly irritating.

"Zane, credit card stuff like this is a victimless crime," Lettie said. She sat on the bed next to Angel, their weight dipping the corner of the thin mattress nearly to the floor. Dust particles puffed into the shaft of late afternoon light coming in through an opening in the curtains. Her face was serious. "The big banks practically budget for these kinds of losses. Individual cardholders rarely pay anything. The credit card companies still make plenty of money with their double-digit interest rates and promises of easy credit."

Zane thought of the video game console he had found in Lettie's room and wondered what more she might have bought. "Next you're going to tell me you donate all the things you buy with those stolen credit cards to the poor, like some kind of Robin Hood character. Lettie and Angel and their merry men."

"Look, Zane, people's personal funds aren't at risk if their credit card is used this way," Angel said. "At the most, it is an inconvenience and maybe about $50 in charges."

Zane wasn't at all convinced, but he decided to back off a bit. Coming too hard at Lettie might drive her away again. He couldn't take the chance. "What kind of money are we talking about here for all those credit card numbers?"

"About $45 a card," Lettie said.

Zane stared back at her, horrified. "Lettie, that's a fortune." He was suddenly aware of the sounds of the motel outside, the rumble of passing cars on the street, the sound of a car door opening and closing in the parking lot. Had he been sure they weren't followed here? He went to the window and plucked the curtain back. No one was in the immediate vicinity but had that white sedan been in the parking lot when they arrived? Lettie and Angel were watching him intently, anticipation on their faces.

"There's no way you're going to get away with stealing that kind of money and go back to your regular lives," Zane said. "You two haven't thought this through." The thought crossed his mind that Angel had been in contact with Lettie this whole time. The two of them had cooked up this scheme and hoped to convince him. The kid was a pretty good actor and liar if that was true, Zane thought.

"But I have been thinking it through, Zane," Lettie said. "I've been doing nothing but thinking it through since Wally Zittman died. It was like a wake-up call to me. He was working with the same people we were and—"

"So you knew him after all?" Zane leaned back against the wall next to the window. It was a lot to take in but he couldn't say he was surprised. Was it possible, he wondered, to be shocked but not surprised?

"Look, Zane, it is possible to go away without being traced. We can go to Mexico—from here we can literally drive across the border. It's like three hours away. We get paid in Bitcoin or one of the cyber currencies. Untraceable. A whole different life. A rebirth. What do we have in Tulsa anyway?"

"Our grandmother, for one," Zane said. "Your father. That's our family. That's our home. You're talking about messing up your whole life, changing everything." He felt a sudden searing homesickness for Oklahoma himself. This room

—this city—felt unfriendly as the twilight outside darkened and yellow parking lots snapped on. He missed the routine of evenings in their apartment and when he thought about the fact he probably had lost both of his jobs to come out here, anxiety pierced his gut.

"Oh, Zane, I'm tired," Lettie said. "Let's talk about this later." She flopped back on the bed to squeaks and groans from the box spring. Angel stretched out next to her and they both shut their eyes.

Worry over them both and the baby consumed him. He sat in a rickety chair with padding so worn it might as well have been wood and leaned his head back against the wall. But after fifteen minutes or so of deep even breathing from Angel and Lettie, his day was catching up with him. The motel room was warm and he was beginning to nod. Low, calm voices from the early evening newscast lulled him to sleep.

He woke with a start a half hour later. His mouth felt like it had a coat of sand and his head was pounding. He went to the bathroom and tore the thin protective covering over the plastic cup, filling the cup with water. Then, realizing he hadn't eaten for hours, he found an old protein bar in his backpack and polished it off along with three cups of water. Feeling more alert, he checked his phone for messages. Nothing new.

He called the number Office Lopez had given him and left her a voicemail that he'd found his sister. He felt safer having the number of an LAPD officer in his phone, even though he knew 911 would probably be faster should anything urgent happen.

As he watched Lettie and Angel sleep, he found himself thinking about his conversation with Bingo the day Lettie took off. Where had Bingo gotten the idea that Lettie was in Catoosa? Why would he even care? He'd never shown that level of interest in their lives before, except as he thought it might make the carnival some money. With everything that had happened over the past week, Zane had been so emotional and anxious that he'd not been suspicious of Bingo. But if anything his past experiences had taught him was to be on alert about anything that might threaten him or Lettie.

As he gazed at the television news weather report—eighty degrees tomorrow, partly cloudy—a glimmer of a half-shaped thought disturbed him. He'd almost grasped it just before he woke up from his nap, he remembered now. Had he been dreaming? Had it been to do with Bingo? He glanced at his phone again and scrolled through the last messages from the carnival boss. Nothing more than a few cursory texts sent during shifts about areas to check out. *"Can you get over to the funnel cake booth? S sez someone is bothering her."* That kind of thing.

The phone screen blacked out, replaced by Ernest Buckskin's name in white letters. Zane moved into the motel room's tiny bathroom to take the video call.

"There you are," he said, and Zane realized it had been weeks since he had talked to his old friend. He looked, Zane thought, as if he'd lost ten pounds since he'd last seen him. Probably the result of the dehydration of a sweat, flesh tight on the bones in his face, maybe made worse by the dark shadows created by some trick of the light. He looked like he was inside his work shed, though it was impossible to tell for sure.

"Do you have time to talk?" Zane could hear the concern in his voice and wondered how the man had such good timing. His voice was a salve over Zane's worries.

"Sure, of course. Things have gotten complicated," Zane said. "I'm in Los Angeles, for one thing."

"What?" Ernest looked baffled for a moment, as if processing the news. "What are you doing there?"

Aware that Lettie and Angel would hear every word he and

Ernest said, Zane kept it simple. He told the other man about the credit card ring, the video of Kevin Perrine killing Wally, how the police were looking for Perrine.

"How are you and Lettie?"

"We're together here," Zane said. He didn't know how to say more. Inside the bathroom, the smell of some kind of floral cleaner, the same brand they used at the zoo, wafted toward him.

"That's good," Ernest said.

"She's pregnant."

"Wonderful news. A new life is always occasion for celebration. Bring her to see us when you are back in Oklahoma," Ernest said.

"She doesn't want to come back," Zane said, watching his own face deepen into a frown on the video screen.

Ernest considered for a moment, looking off-camera at something. "Every one of us has a thread running through our lives. A trajectory that slowly arcs toward the good, I believe. You have it. Lettie has it. I have it. You have to believe that the pull of that thread is the right one."

Zane nodded, reluctantly. "I'm not sure what I believe."

"You do know, you just have to take time and sit with your thoughts. Maybe Lettie does too."

Chapter Twenty-Five

Zane left the two of them napping in the motel to get food. The taco stand about half a mile down Lankershim Boulevard looked like a family-run establishment. A woman's face framed by flowing black hair stared at the cracks in the parking lot pavement from a mural painted on the side of a square and squat building. The guy working at the motel front desk had said it was a much better option than the McDonald's down the road and cheaper than the trendy ramen and vegan places that dotted the North Hollywood arts district.

The scent of spiced meat drew growls from Zane's hungry stomach. Inside, a menu hung above a counter fronted with plexiglass. A man in a white T-shirt stood over a grill full of chicken and beef. A polished cement floor led to a courtyard in the back with a small bricked area with worn plastic and metal furniture. Strings of twinkling lights adorned the tops of the walls inside and stretched above the outdoor seating area. A plaintive ballad rang out from a speaker somewhere.

The restaurant was so small, Zane hesitated at the entrance —it seemed almost an intrusion to walk into such an intimate space. He wondered if he would be expected to speak Spanish to order, and he racked his brain for some phrases from that sophomore year language class. But the man behind the counter turned around and welcomed him in English with a big smile, sparing him the dilemma.

"What can I make for you?"

Zane scanned the menu, which stretched nearly six feet long above the man's head. Tacos and burritos with six different meat options, three different tortilla options, breakfast burritos, chalupas, tostadas, nachos. The menu was overwhelming but the smell of the meat made up his mind for him. He ordered the family taco meal, all chicken tacos.

The man got to work. The food here was definitely not of the fast, prepared in advance kind. Zane watched him cook for a while, then let the heat of the un-air-conditioned space slowly relax him. He would talk Lettie off of this cliff. The best thing to do would be to go to Old Spice and tell him what had happened. He could count on him to help them out and keep Lettie out of as much trouble as he could. Surely her cooperation would mean something to the law-and-order types. For Zane, it felt like the baby changed everything. She had to see that the "run to Mexico" plan was foolish and that stealing what could be millions of dollars would put a target on her back for the rest of her life. She seemed to have technical skills to evade scrutiny, but how long could she keep that up?

He grabbed the white plastic bag full of food and headed back to the car. He remembered seeing a drug store nearby when they had driven to Emmaline's apartment and decided to go get some aspirin for the headache he felt coming on. A big gallon of water might be a good idea, too, he thought. He wasn't sure he trusted the water coming from the tap at that motel.

Streetlights flickered on and the remains of a stunning red-orange sunset lingered behind the strip mall kitty-corner the drug store. The light of the city had gone soft and gold, making the cars and buildings at the intersection seem filtered and soft-focus. As he walked through the automatic sliding doors of the store, he thought he caught the faintest whiff of star jasmine in the air. Coming towards him was Emmaline, holding a plastic bag and wearing big sunglasses despite the sunset. Her face was white as chalk and the look she gave Zane was wary.

"What timing," said Emmaline. Zane noticed a bruise turning purple just under her sunglasses, and his uneasiness plummeted to dread.

"What happened to you? Are you all right?"

"I'm fine," she said, shaking her head. Her hand fluttered to the sunglasses, touching the frame lightly. "I slipped and fell, silly me."

"Let me see," he said. She shook her head, her hair moving off of her neck to shown what looked like the imprint of two fingers on the tender skin.

They stepped to the side near a rack of souvenir North Hollywood T-shirts to let a couple of customers pass through the doors. The only way Zane could visualize Emmaline getting that kind of bruising from a fall would be if she'd fallen directly on her eye and then decided to strangle herself.

"You need to leave him," Zane said. "It's not worth it. Come back with us."

"It's not that simple," she said.

"It is that simple," he argued. "If you're worried about the money, don't be. I can help." It would mean more credit card debt and less savings, but what else could he do? Emmaline may be a disappointment as a friend, but she was more like family. And family members sometimes let you down, but you don't turn your back on them.

"I wish you hadn't come here to see this," she said. "I wanted you all to think of me as successful out here."

"You had us fooled, that's for sure," Zane said. "But what is the point of all that pretending online? Trying to present your life like it is some television show or something, it's silly. It doesn't matter what other people think. It matters what you think. Are you even happy out here?"

Her smile was rueful. "You don't understand," she said. "I can't go back there and give up. It might still happen for me. Hope is born every day out here."

Zane shook his head. "I don't like seeing you like this. Neither would your parents. Nothing's worth this kind of treatment."

"I fell, Zane." Her answer was flat, final, her clamped lips making it clear she meant it.

But she was lying.

Back at the motel, a few more cars filled the parking lot and Zane had trouble finding a space near Lettie's room. One black SUV with tinted windows was taking up two spots, a selfish act that drove Zane nuts even when parking lots were relatively empty instead of full like this one was now.

His headache had only intensified since seeing Emmaline, a white-hot spot of pain throbbing behind his right eye. Clearly she wanted to stay in Los Angeles with Colt and had no problem lying about what was going on. But that didn't make it right for him to do nothing. He considered calling her parents. He knew they would drop everything to come out here and talk some sense into her. But was it his place to interfere so heavily in her life? She was an adult who made her own choices. But she was obviously in harm's way. His thoughts continued to circle as he sat in the car, head aching and stomach grumbling. He needed to eat. So did Lettie and Angel. The car clock said it was just past seven.

He rapped on the motel room door and after what seemed like an interminable wait, a man in his fifties answered the door. He was short, slightly stocky, with buzzcut grey hair and wore a green plaid button-down shirt with the sleeves rolled up, showing off a black tattoo.

"Sorry," Zane said, backing up to take another look at the motel room number. "I must have the wrong room."

"Zane Clearwater?" The man reached into his shirt pocket and Zane had the impulse to drop the tacos and run. Had the goons from Tulsa somehow found them here? Over the man's shoulder, he could see Lettie sitting on the edge of the bed, laptop perched on her knees. A woman with thick, shoulder length hair sat next to her, peering at the screen.

The man held out a badge. The letters FBI swam in front of Zane's eyes. He knew he should try to read the badge, make sure it was real, but he was too stunned to make sense of the words on it.

"I'm Doug Oliphant with the FBI," the man said. "Why don't you come in and we can talk?"

Zane slipped into the room and set the tacos on the dresser. Angel jumped up from the armchair by the window and tore into the plastic bag. "I'm starving," he said. Zane was surprised. His own appetite had completely died again, though the headache remained, pounding out a warning signal behind his eye that seemed to make the whole room pulse. The woman stood up and reached out her hand. "I'm Melanie Strom," she said. "Also an FBI agent."

Her eyes locked on his in a guarded but probing expression that made him want to measure every word and action. He shook her hand, or rather she shook his, a woman used to hustling people past uncertainty and into action.

"What's going on?" he said. She looked like a television version of an FBI agent even without the badge for proof. Her posture was ramrod straight, her brown hair slicked back in a ponytail, her starched white shirt tucked too tightly into black pants. No jewelry other than a thin silver chain around her neck.

"You must be Zane, Lettie's brother," she said. He didn't like the feeling of having walked into a scene already underway. He felt like an actor who had forgotten his lines, with all of the other players expecting him to do or say something to move the scene forward.

"Go ahead and eat before your food gets cold," she said, nodding at the bag, but her gesture was perfunctory.

Lettie set the laptop down and rose from the bed to get a taco as Angel dug in. "I'm starving," she said.

"What is going on?" Zane repeated.

"Your sister is in a bit of trouble," Strom said.

"No shit."

"No need to be a smart ass," she said, obviously not appreciating his outburst. With a frown, she leaned toward him. "We know about the credit card numbers she has been trying to sell."

Zane blinked. "I figured as much. So are you here to arrest her?"

"That all depends."

Ah. Light dawned. Lettie was too small-time for them. Too easy. But potentially useful.

"Your sister knows some very bad people."

Duh, Zane thought. But with that first reaction came another: a pang of guilt over what he feared was his inadequate supervision of Lettie. He swallowed it down with effort. He looked at his sister, nibbling at a taco as she sat on the edge of the bed, watching him talk to the agent. He saw misplaced teenage confidence in her face, the assumption she could come out on top no matter what. He looked for fear in her eyes but was more disturbed to find excitement.

"Zane," Lettie said. "This might be a better plan than—" She let her voice trail off but he knew what she meant. The pipe dream of the escape to Mexico, the million-dollar payout. The life as a criminal fugitive with dangerous enemies. This change of heart was some relief.

"Depends on what, exactly?" he said carefully.

"Depends on her cooperation, which she assures me we have. Do we have yours?" Strom said.

Zane bristled. "You're going to need to tell me more than you have so far."

"We have been tracking this credit card theft ring for months. We knew about your sister's involvement on the fringes, basic stuff. Her and her friend Angel here are bit players. But things have been heating up since Wally Zittman was killed. Lots of drama, infighting. Then, surprise! Your sister steals the motherlode and heads off to Los Angeles. We weren't sure what her endgame was. She knows enough to hide her tracks pretty well from the bad guys but at the FBI we have better tools than they do. So we moved in today. We want Lettie to reinitiate contact with them."

"Too dangerous," Zane blurted out. "No way."

"It is not more dangerous than trying to sell those numbers to persons unknown and fleeing the country."

"I wasn't going to let her do that," Zane said. "I was working on a plan."

"Let us help you," Agent Oliphant said. "We can keep her safe."

Zane wanted to believe the man, but the sick feeling in his stomach told him the promise came too easy. He felt like Oliphant was playing the scripted role of good cop to Strom's bad cop, meant to put him more at ease in an uncomfortable, awful situation. He was being manipulated. First by Angel and Lettie, now by these FBI agents. He didn't like it. But he didn't have a choice but to go along with this new plan. If he was honest with himself, he wasn't exactly brimming full of ideas of what to do next, other than get Lettie back to Tulsa and turn the credit card numbers over to the Tulsa police. This was practically the same idea, except he didn't know these FBI agents and wasn't sure he could trust them as much as he would trust Old Spice.

"I take it we'd go back to Tulsa, right?" Zane said. Oliphant and Strom nodded.

"Okay, then," he said. "What else?"

Chapter Twenty-Six

Zane woke feeling anxious as well as stiff from sleeping on a rollaway bed, which was six inches too short for him. Lettie was sitting up in bed, scrolling her phone, while Angel snored beside her. Zane couldn't believe he had managed to sleep through the sound, which was loud as a train.

"He ought to get checked out for that sleep apnea thing," Zane said to Lettie. He rose and grabbed a water bottle from the dresser and took a long swig.

Lettie grunted without taking her eyes off of the screen. "Emmaline's posts seem so pathetic now that we've seen what's going on there," she said. "I've been scrolling through the old posts this morning, looking for clues I should have seen. There's nothing, other than just that it all seems too perfectly curated. A charmed life."

Zane opened the taco bag from the night before and pulled out a tortilla chip. It had turned soft and greasy overnight but he ate it anyway.

"I ran into her at the drug store before I came back here last night. She looked banged up. Black eye."

"What?" Lettie let the phone drop to her lap. Angel stirred in his sleep, the snoring mercifully halted as he turned on his side.

"She said she fell."

"And you believed that?"

"Of course not. But she insisted. You know how she gets. I asked her to come home with us but she said everything was fine."

"That's crazy. We ought to go over there and take her by force. Smack that boyfriend Colt, pack her bags and put her on the plane with us." His sister's insistence and sense of moral justice reminded him of himself, but she hadn't seen the stubbornness in Emmaline's eyes. She'd never admit she was in trouble, not to them, let alone flee the city to run back to Tulsa. He told his sister as much but his words only riled Lettie more.

"What do you mean, just give up on her? Leave her here for this guy to hurt some more?"

"She's an adult," Zane said. "I let her know I was here for her. She told me she didn't need our help. Other than kidnap her, what can we do?"

Lettie got out of bed and shoved her phone screen into his face. "Look at this post. Is this a cry for help or what?"

The post was from very early this morning. The photo showed a window, but the focus was on the weave of the metal window screen. The golden yellow light of sunrise was blurred in the background as was the window frame.

"She's taking photos of window screens, for heaven's sake, Zane," Lettie said. "Like a caged animal. And look at the captions: "#newdaydawning #makeitcount #liveyourbestlife."

"Honestly, it sounds like the same kind of babble she's always posting. And the window screen thing, that's just her idea of artsy."

"At six a.m.? She never posts at six a.m. I'm telling you, this is a call for help."

Lettie's insistence stirred his own sense of duty to his old friend. Maybe she did need rescuing. Maybe he just hadn't been persuasive enough when he ran into her at the drugstore. He had been so overtaken by surprise and anger he hadn't said the right things to make her come to her senses. She had to be looking for an out—Colt had told them her career wasn't going anywhere anytime soon and he certainly wasn't any good reason for her to stick around this city. He also had to admit that he liked the idea of being her hero—and his sister's. The past week had been frustrating and scary. Helping Emmaline seemed like something he could do. A quick glance at his watch confirmed there would be time enough before their flight to Tulsa to make a stop. Once they got back to Tulsa, the hard part would start as Lettie would have to try to get her job back with the credit card ring and then inform on them to the FBI.

"All right, let's go by there on our way to the airport," he said.

Chapter Twenty-Seven

They had decided to execute a surprise attack, showing up at the door of the apartment unannounced. Zane rapped on the door with his knuckles, loud like a cop would. It was nine a.m. and the knock rang out loud in the quiet courtyard. Plastic vertical blinds shifted in windows around them but no faces appeared.

He hit the door again and this time called out her name. This drew a response. He heard heavy footsteps from inside the apartment, small voices rising. Emmaline's anxious soprano against Colt's barked rhythm. He felt Angel and Emmaline back up slightly, their bravery vanishing a bit in light of the anger they could sense in the way Colt pulled the door open like an explosion.

"What. The. Fuck. Do. You. Want."

Zane faced Colt, not moving an inch, looking down a half-foot at him. Colt locked his eyes upward, hands at his sides, clenched in fists. Behind him, Zane could hear Lettie's breath coming fast.

"Where's Emmaline?"

"She's putting on her clothes," Colt said, baring his teeth in a wolf's smile.

"We want to talk to her," Zane said. "Alone."

Colt's eyes left his and flickered to the left. "Are you shooting video?" Colt said.

"You betcha," Lettie said, stretching her arm out so the phone's camera was closer to his face.

Colt fell silent, his angry impulses tempered by the presence of the camera. His body gave up the fighter's stance and he shifted to the side, back against the wall. The power of bullies always seemed strong until it crumbled, Zane thought. Colt's vacillation between violence and submission wasn't surprising, but he remained wary, not sure how long it would last. He'd known enough bullies on the playground and work to see the pattern. The muscles in Zane's legs twitched, ready to spring forward.

"What do you all want?"

Emmaline appeared like a ghost from the shadows of the apartment in white sweatpants pooling around pale ankles and bare feet and a white sweatshirt a few sizes too big. One blue eye looked deep-set and drooping, the other peered out from a halo of skin puffed around it like a reddish-purple ravioli. As Zane contemplated his options, he heard Lettie take in a sharp breath behind him. He thought about what his sponsor would say, what Ernest Buckskin would say, even what his mother would have suggested. They would all have undoubtedly mature and sensible advice about the power of heart-to-heart conversations and showing Emmaline she had his support when she was ready to leave. But that calm outlook just refused to extend to his fists, which were clenching by his side. All he wanted to do was give Colt a shiner to match Emmaline's. Maybe even two.

Colt's thick biceps and forearms showed he spent some

time in the gym. Zane still thought he could win a fight with the guy, or at least land a few really good punches. He doubted Colt had spent much time using those vanity muscles for anything other than posing in the mirror or showing off how much he could lift. A real man would never hit a woman, he thought. No, hitting Emmaline was the work of a real asshole.

"Go ahead, hit me," Colt said. "Let's go." He pushed Emmaline back into the apartment and came at Zane over the threshold. "I can see it all over your face, you wanting to come to the rescue to your old love. She told me all about it, your undying love for her, the pathetic way you hung around her, begging for scraps."

"Colt, shut up!" Emmaline said.

"At least I really care about her," said Zane. He mentally calibrated the distance from his right fist to Colt's chin.

"This isn't helping me," Emmaline said, but Zane wasn't sure if she was talking to him or Colt or Lettie and Angel.

"Em, seriously, what are you doing with this guy? Come back with us, we'll figure it out," Lettie said.

"I don't know," Emmaline said. Her faltering drew Colt's attention and he studied her with narrowed eyes. Zane saw an opportunity. He coiled his shoulder muscles, drew a deep breath and slammed his right fist into Colt's face. The punch hit, but not with the bone-on-bone impact Zane expected from connecting with the jawbone. Instead his fist landed on cartilage and soft tissue. He'd smashed Colt's nose dead-on.

Bright red blood began to flow around Colt's hands, which were now steepled over his nose. "You goddamn asshole, you had to punch my face," he said. "I've got a fucking audition in two days." He tossed his head back, eyes on the ceiling. "Get me a towel, Emmaline."

Zane had expected the man to fight back. He stayed in a

fighter's stance, alert for a surprise attack. Maybe Colt was just faking him out.

But Emmaline returned with a dark brown towel from the bathroom and Colt flopped onto the couch, his head still back and eyes on the ceiling.

"Got enough video already?" Emmaline held her hand up to Lettie's phone camera. "Why don't you send me that and I'll show it to the police. How Zane just came in here and punched my boyfriend."

Lettie lowered the camera. "He provoked him and you know it," she said. "Come on, Emmaline, just come with us."

Emmaline pivoted to the kitchen and opened the freezer door. She brought a sack of frozen peas over to the couch and tried to move the towel aside from Colt's face. He brushed her away.

"Em—I'm sorry it's happening like this," Zane said. "We're leaving. You can too."

"I'm good," she said. At this, Colt peeked at them from behind the towel pressed to his face. Rivulets of blood had dried around his fingers like a hideous tattoo. He moved the towel away just enough to let them see his nasty, self-satisfied smile.

Chapter Twenty-Eight

Zane smelled the sharp tang of sulfur in the car and immediately accused Angel of letting one rip. "Roll the windows down, man," he said.

"Don't!" Lettie said from the backseat. He glanced in the rearview mirror to see her holding a pink candle in glass on her lap. The faint odor of herbs and flowers made its way to his nose.

"What are you doing?"

"I'm setting a protection spell for us," Lettie said.

"Don't you need a pentagram or an altar or something?" Angel asked.

"A talented witch can do magic anywhere," Lettie said. "The guy at the Bloodrose told me he could do it from a restaurant table and no one would even know it."

Zane wouldn't argue with her. They could use all the protection they could get.

"I'm really glad you're not going to Mexico," Zane said.

"I haven't ruled it out," Lettie said.

"Being on the run isn't like a vacation," Zane said. His

mind drifted back to the crude log cabin his father Jeremiah Doom had let him hide in last year when Zane was running from the law. The deep silence of the days, the hours that stretched so long, the musty smell. He woke up every morning there with a hard ball of anxiety in his stomach. Rightly so, he reflected. He had taken a very wrong path and Jeremiah hadn't had his best interests at heart. Zane definitely wanted the best for Lettie but making her see and understand that was so difficult.

"Being a snitch for the FBI isn't all that fun either," Lettie said.

"A snitch? Don't say that, Lettie. You're doing the right thing. Don't believe that the stuff you see in the movies about codes of honor between criminals. There are no codes of honor. The people who decide to break the law like this—professionally, I mean—they are just in it for themselves. They'd turn you in too. Those kinds of people would sell you out in a heartbeat."

"It's true," Angel said. "My mother always says that the only thing worse than being lied to is not knowing that you're being lied to. She said Kevin Perrine and his friends were liars but that didn't mean you couldn't do business with them. You just had to know what you were getting into."

Zane's affection for Angel had been growing since Lettie ran away, because he'd seen how the teenager really cared for his sister. But that comment made him mad. If it weren't for Angel and Angel's mom and their stupid idea about making money off of credit card fraud, they wouldn't be in this trouble. The kid may be sweet but he didn't always have good judgment, that was for sure.

Zane inched the rental car into the intersection, waiting for a large group of office workers and a few people in workout clothes to finish crossing the street. They all seemed to be heading toward the Starbucks on the corner. A bright blue sedan behind him sat on his tail and the driver leaned on the horn.

When Zane glanced at the driver in his rear-view mirror, his stomach flopped. He recognized him. It was Kevin Perrine. He was holding the steering wheel in both hands, wearing dark sunglasses so big they looked like he'd stolen them from a movie star in the 1970s, and a dark knit cap pulled low. Zane debated whether he should tell Lettie and Angel, but when Perrine held his hand out of the window and gestured that he should pull over, Zane figured he had to. After all, he'd have to make the choice: fight or flight.

The last of the pedestrians crossed the street, clearing a space for Zane's left turn onto Lankershim. Cars lined the broad street at every meter. There wasn't anywhere to pull over even if he wanted to.

"Kevin Perrine's behind us," he said. Angel and Lettie twisted around in one motion. Lettie turned back to the front, clutched the candle and began mumbling something under her breath.

"This isn't part of the plan. Should we call the FBI?" Angel said. His words tumbled out in a high-pitched rush.

Zane made the turn with Perrine on his tail, only to be taken by surprise when the other man screeched out from behind him and then suddenly cut back in front, forcing Zane to hit the brakes. Traffic began to pile up behind them and a cacophony of horns erupted. Perrine pulled forward, his hand rising above the roof of the car and pointing toward the right side of the street.

"Angel, find out where the nearest police station is," Lettie said. "Then drive there."

Zane pulled forward as Perrine held back, intent on following instead of leading. An office building parking garage entrance loomed on the right side and Zane considered turning into it and begging the parking attendant to call the cops. But it seemed doomed to fail—Perrine would just follow him in and even if the police were called, they wouldn't arrive fast enough to stop anything from happening. There was no way to know if Perrine was armed, but Zane assumed he was. The thought of him even threatening to hurt Lettie or Angel terrified him.

In the rearview mirror he saw Lettie, eyes shut, gripping the candle she had lit for protection, her face still and breath deep. Next to him, Angel's breathing had quickened and his hands shook as he swiped at his phone. "The police station is the other way," he said.

Then Zane saw it.

Ahead, parked in front of a bank, was a black and white police car, red lights flashing. Two officers stood on the sidewalk, talking to a white dude with dreadlocks and a large boombox strapped to his bike's handlebars. Zane made a quick right into the narrow driveway of the bank parking lot and then drove headlong across the sidewalk toward the cops, who turned around and glared. He stopped about five feet from them and held up his hands.

Perrine's rental car rolled past like a fat blue marble, then merged into the flow of cars on Lankershim.

Chapter Twenty-Nine

The flight home was uneventful. With Kevin Perrine's face plastered all over TSA computer screens Zane felt like he could relax a bit. The man who killed Wally Zittman wasn't likely to pop up unexpectedly any more today. By tomorrow, they'd have their plan in action with Gene and the threat Perrine posed would be neutralized. Hopefully. A lot had to happen before then.

They arrived in Tulsa at dinnertime. Zane's stomach growled at the smell from the barbecue place next to the gate where they landed. As if of one mind, the three of them paused in front of the place and stared at the menu hanging on the wall behind the counter.

"Twelve dollars for a brisket sandwich," Zane scoffed. "A whole chicken doesn't cost twelve dollars."

"I've got money," Angel said. Zane had to laugh. The kid had been trying to pay for things the whole trip and he hadn't let him. He suspected that money came from the credit card fraud ring and he wanted to set an example for them. Though the more he thought about it, the sillier it seemed. What he was showing them was how easy it was to sink into credit card debt. Zane wasn't even sure he could get either of his jobs back.

"Sure, let's do it," Zane said.

They joined the line-up behind a woman with brown hair and a starched blue shirt with the Southwest logo stitched on the pocket.

She turned around and smiled at him. "You found your sister," she said.

Zane was about to ask her how she knew, but Lettie asked first.

"He came looking for you," she said. "He was so worried. I prayed you two would be reunited."

"Thanks for the prayers, then," Zane said. He introduced himself and Lettie and Angel.

"I'm Marlene," she said. "Remember, I sold you your ticket."

Lettie nodded.

"I got in a little trouble with my supervisor that day. Telling me that I shouldn't be giving out information on our passengers and all that."

"Sorry to hear that," Zane said. "It made a big difference to us. We knew we were on the right track."

"I told her that it wasn't like we were doctors or lawyers or something. We are ticket agents. There's no right to privacy oath I took."

She plucked a bottle of lemon tea out of the refrigerated bin and sighed. Her red-white-and-blue manicure rat-tat-tatted on the glass. Then she leaned toward him, neck stretching stiffly, like a rheumatic vulture.

"See anyone over the age of fifteen can buy a ticket just like an adult, it's as simple as that. I don't necessarily agree that every fifteen or sixteen-year-old is mature enough to be making an unsupervised trip like that to a den of sin like Los Angeles.

So close to the Mexican border and those sex traffickers who take girls and do you-know-what to," Marlene said.

The line was moving really slow, Zane thought. The man at the front of the line had just asked if he could pay with PayPal instead of a credit card.

"I wouldn't let my daughter out of my sight when she was her age," Marlene said, her eyes flicking to where Lettie stood looking at her phone. If only this woman knew, Zane thought.

Lettie, perhaps sensing that an interruption would be welcome, cleared her throat. "Restaurant rater says this is the worst barbecue place in Tulsa," she said. "Literally they've ranked them from one to fifty-two and this place is fifty-two."

"There aren't a lot of great options here," Marlene said. "But I come here because the staff are, you know, All-American."

Zane gave a closer look at the woman behind the counter, half-expecting to see some kind of athletic type or pageant queen who would rate the All-American title. But the woman working the register looked like her special talent was more likely to be chewing gum than baton twirling or the long jump. Pasty white skin, acne-scarred cheeks, stringy hair the color of dirt, jaw moving slowly on a piece of bright pink gum as she told the man for the third time it was credit card or cash only. She looked bored out of her mind.

"Over at the hamburger place, I can barely understand a word any of them say," Marlene added, but he got her racist message loud and clear without the clarification.

He considered telling her that the title of All-American might in fact belong to those who occupied the land well before European settlers arrived, but the PayPal dude had finally paid for his sandwich with a combination of crumpled dollars and another credit card, clearing the path for Marlene to order.

As she waited for the so-called All-American woman to get

her chicken sandwich, Marlene turned back to Zane one last time.

"I forgot to ask," she said. "Did your uncle catch up with you all in Los Angeles?"

"My uncle?"

"Yeah—dark haired guy, kind of paunchy if you know what I mean. Said his name was Bob something," she said.

Zane exchanged glances with Angel and Lettie. She wasn't describing Wally Zittman or Gene. Maybe it was one of the FBI agents?

"Oh, yeah, um, he found us," Zane said.

"That's good," she said. "Family needs to stick together."

Chapter Thirty

The air-conditioning was on the fritz again in the car. Heat from a day's worth of sunshine had accumulated, making the car toasty warm even though the evening temperature was a balmy sixty-five degrees. Warm, chemical-scented air flowed around them as they rolled down the windows.

Tulsa in the twilight seemed provincial and slow, only two other cars on their side of the highway as orange streetlights flickered to life. As Zane accelerated to the highway speed limit, he flipped through the radio dial until he landed on a news station.

A nasal twang rang through the speakers. "It's the cancel culture, you know, people try to make their views known and Big Tech shuts them down. People don't like your opinion and they just don't want to hear it so they shut you down."

And then the radio host. "What you can't forget, Bob, is that tens of millions of people are voting for this. Unity under fascism. Unity is you better agree or you are up the creek. It's a demand that you agree with your political opponents or else. It's not pretty. It's not pleasant but that's how it is."

Zane glanced in the rearview mirror at Lettie as she stared out the window. "Did you call to let the agent know we arrived?"

His sister popped her head between the front seats. "Was I supposed to?"

"Yes," Zane said. "You have to keep them informed."

If he was being honest with himself, he worried that these plans they had made would backfire. Had they made a choice that brought them into more danger than they needed to be? The FBI agents and their reassurances seemed very far away as he drove I-44 in the deepening darkness toward the apartment.

Lettie slid back and picked up the phone. Her voice was a low murmur as she left a message. Zane turned up the radio, where a woman was quoting the Bible. "He who plans a thing will be successful; happy is he who trusts in the Lord," the woman's voice said. "So this spring, plan for a beautiful yard that is easy to maintain with a Kubota riding lawnmower."

A sudden surge of air conditioned cool from the car's vents made his sweat go cold as their highway exit approached on the right. This was not the time to take Lettie home.

"Hey, you're going to miss the exit," Angel said, pointing out the window. Zane pressed the gas harder as 21st Street exit whizzed by.

"I'm taking you all to our grandmother's," he said. "And this time, Lettie, you're going to stay there for a while. I've got some stuff I need to do."

Chapter Thirty-One

The evening air felt damp as Zane stretched himself out of the parked car in front of their grandmother's house. The two-hour drive had left him stiff and a little jumpy. Or maybe it was just latent fear of their situation, the worry about being back in Oklahoma, the question of where Kevin Perrine was now, and who else Gene had sent looking for them.

In the street, he heard little crickets rasping in the weeds along the curb, a streetlight humming. From inside the house, came the sound of a door opening and his name and Lettie's shouted from the porch.

"Grandma!" Lettie was shouting back and running toward her.

"Don't knock her down," Zane called out, laughing. He found he couldn't wait to throw his arms around his grandma either.

They hugged and then they hugged some more, crowded onto the porch. Angel hung back a little bit until Verda caught his eye and called him over too.

"After I'm done hugging you all I'm gonna whip your behinds," Verda said. "Just for making me worry so."

"I'm so sorry, Grandma," Lettie said. "I'm sorry I left without saying goodbye."

"Don't you know that I've always got your back, Lettie? You can tell me anything," Verda said and Zane felt his own tears rise to match the ones he saw in Lettie's eyes.

Verda shuffled them into the kitchen through the stacks of paper and containers. Still, he saw Lettie cringe a little, turning to read Angel's first reaction to the piles and piles of paper and junk. Angel moved through the hoarder's pathway without a second glance. Zane appreciated the kid's accepting attitude. An unintended benefit of the way he was raised, no doubt. He'd seen the worst at home, so other people's weirdness didn't faze him at all. Lettie seemed to relax a bit as Angel lifted a stack of junk mail off of one of the chairs and gestured for her to sit.

"I've got some chili I can heat up," Verda said. "I'm guessing you're hungry." The barbecue sandwich seemed so long ago, so Zane nodded along with Lettie and Angel.

"I'm pregnant," Lettie blurted out.

Verda had just opened the refrigerator door and paused for a moment, staring into the shelves, white light shining on her face. Zane waited for the reaction, annoyed with Lettie for the impulse to deliver the news in such an impactful, dramatic way. He had no idea what Verna's reaction would be. Would she would blame him for not keeping a good enough eye on her?

Verda pulled a big yellow covered plastic dish out of the refrigerator and set it on the counter. She looked tired for an instant, but then a smile erased the weariness from her face.

"How wonderful!" Verda said. "I'm going to be a great-grandmother."

"You already are a great grandmother," Lettie said, hitting hard on the word great and smiling.

"Yeah, exactly!"

Verda laughed and it was a genuine laugh. Sitting here around their grandmother's cluttered kitchen table, surrounded by the faded wallpaper and stacks of mail and cereal boxes and cans of beans and soup, they felt like a family, Angel included. He would do everything he could to protect them. He owed them that. In the end, family—connected by blood or love—was all you really had, he thought.

Later as Lettie and Angel napped in the bedroom, Zane found his grandmother in her chair by the kitchen stove, looking at old photos behind yellowed plastic sheets in a ring-bound album.

"Aren't you tired?" she asked.

"No," he said.

But he was tired and he realized looking at his grandmother's face that she looked tired too. She struggled to peel back the acetate sheet off of the album page, pink fingernails scratching at it to no avail. "Come here and look at this picture of your mother when she was pregnant with you."

Zane bent slowly and peered at the snapshot, resisting the temptation to pinch and squeeze it to make his mother's face bigger as you would on a smart phone screen. Its 1980s colors were faded now, the floral wallpaper behind her a wash of green and blue behind his mother's mulleted perm and her bubblegum pink crop top emblazoned with the Pony logo. She must have been in the early stages of the pregnancy, because Zane couldn't detect any sign of a swollen belly.

"Who took that picture?"

"Her daddy did. It's funny now to think about that day. It was a few weeks before she took off to make her clean break from us and Jeremiah. Osbert had some unused film in the camera from our trip to Eureka Springs, Arkansas, and said he wanted to use it up so he snapped some photos of us in the kitchen."

Her fingernail tapped on the photo below his mother's, where Verda herself stood smiling in what looked like the same spot his mother's image had occupied. She had on a red and yellow apron, her head was cocked to one side, and her eyebrows raised.

"I didn't think nothing of it at the time," she said. "But now I wonder if he had a sense, you know, that she would leave. People say mothers have these unbreakable bonds with their kids, but Osbert had something special with your mama Lily. Maybe he knew this would be the last photograph we'd have of her. And now I know that you were growing inside her when it was taken."

Her hand reached out to smooth the hair over his ear. He straightened up and took her in, how watery her blue irises looked, the creases set deep in the corners of her eyes.

"I don't know why she thought we wouldn't help her," Verda said. "I don't know what I could have said to her that made her think she had to go raise you on her own."

"You said it before, she was trying to make a clean break with everything. She wanted to get away from Jeremiah."

"But she could have trusted us."

He leaned in to give Verda a kiss on the cheek, not knowing what else to say. He hadn't realized before that Lettie's running away while pregnant echoed his own mother's flight from danger.

"I'd let you have this photo but it looks like it's stuck permanently in this album," Verda said. "Maybe Lettie would like to see it."

"Definitely."

"I guess y'all could have the album if you wanted, but some of it's just me and Osbert taking our vacation snaps. You ever been to Eureka Springs?"

Zane shook his head.

"They've got this 65-foot tall statue of Jesus there called Christ of the Ozarks. In the summer they do a play about Jesus's last days. We went once to see it."

She flipped the album pages backward and pointed to a photo of the statue. It was a modern, simplified Jesus, arms stretched out, eyes open, face serene.

"I've never been out of Oklahoma til now," Zane said. "I used to beg Mom just to take us to Silver Dollar City in Branson."

"Osbert and I took your mom there, way back before they had the water park and all that. They had a rollercoaster and a lot of these craftsmen demonstrating how to do things like blacksmith. It's a whole big complex now."

"Going to Los Angeles would have seemed so out of reach. Now I've been there and back and you know what? It isn't very nice."

"Anything you build up can be a letdown," Verda said. "Besides, you were there on a mission to find your sister. You weren't there to see the sights."

"Saw some of Hollywood, anyway," Zane said. "I bet Branson's nicer than that."

Verda chuckled. "Maybe so."

She ran her hands over the photos one more time as though caressing the memories they held. And then she closed the album.

"Verda—Grandma—I'm sorry."

She looked startled. "What for?"

"Because Lettie got pregnant. Because she's in trouble and I didn't watch out for her. You...you must be disappointed in me. In her. I should have known better. And now she's in trouble with the law too and the FBI's involved and I'm not sure how we're all going to get out of this."

Verda leaned forward, thrusting her head into Zane's ring of personal space. Her hands reached out and grabbed his arms tight. "What is there to be disappointed in? I have a grandson and a granddaughter I didn't know I had and they have very interesting lives. So much more interesting than anything I see on reality shows. So there's some trouble that has to be sorted out. Life is just a series of different kinds of trouble that has to be sorted out. That's what this daily march is all about."

"Really?"

"Yes, really. 100 percent, like that emoji Lettie texts me."

"Okay then."

"Everything's going to be okay, Zane. We'll get through this. This is my redemption too, you know. Your mother thought she had to do everything on her own. She underestimated just how much love there is my heart and I'm not gonna let you do that."

"But...really?"

She looked at him, nodding. Her fingers squeezed his arms again.

"Thank you, Gramma."

"It's nothing," she said.

That night, tucked under blankets on his grandmother's couch, Zane picked up his phone and scrolled through the contacts in his text messages. It was a list of all the people who were important to him—Lettie, Verda, Ernest, Old Spice, Angel, even Bingo Pratt and Gerry. Some people were blessed with a large family full of blood relations, and some people built their families day by day from the people around them. The horrible way his father and stepbrothers had treated him and Lettie bore witness that blood didn't necessarily mean love or loyalty. The old hatred toward them rose up in him. But he didn't want to let that grab hold of him at his grandmother's house, with her affection surrounding him and Lettie. All you could do is march forward, he thought. His scrolling fingers stopped and pressed on Tiffany's name, remembering her bracelets jangling as she input his mobile number into her phone at the carnival. Had that only been a few days ago? So much had happened.

Even though it was late, he started typing a text to her. Without thinking about it much, he wrote: *Back in Tulsa from L.A. Crazy story to tell you.*

He hit send and almost immediately regretted it. Would she think he was trying to hook up tonight? Why didn't he write *Crazy story to tell you* **sometime**? Late night texts from random guys were always interpreted as booty calls. What was he thinking? He flung the phone on the floor and stared at the ceiling for a few moments.

Then his phone dinged. He knew with a warm rush that it was her responding. He tapped the message icon, holding his breath.

Tiffany: *What happened??? Los Angeles??? Tell me everything!*

Zane woke up, eyes still closed. Angel was on the phone in the kitchen, whispering.

"But that's not right. That's not right."

He lay very still, listening.

"But why would we go to Little Rock now?"

By the sound of his voice, Angel was standing in the kitchen with his back to the living room. Zane opened his eyes.

"I can't come back just yet."

Angel sat in Verda's chair by the stove, holding a half-eaten peach in his hand.

"You should go. Don't worry about me. I'll catch up to you."

Angel took a bite of the fruit. Zane watched him chew slowly like a cow, then stop abruptly.

"You don't need to worry about me, Mom." A brief pause, and then he said, "I've got a plan and you're going to have to trust me," with the finality of a parent speaking to a child, not the other way around. After putting the phone down on his lap, he sat as though waiting for the conversation to continue. Zane didn't move either. Could they trust Angel's mother? How much had Angel just told her about what was going on? She was the one who got them into the carding ring in the first place. Who knows what her involvement might be?

It was another wrinkle he'd have to tell those FBI agents about today when they met, along with handing over the Black-Berry phone they'd found in Zittman's trailer.

Angel stood up and tossed the peach core into the trash and washed his hands at the sink over a stack of refreezable ice blocks and a package of chicken thighs Verda had taken out of the freezer the night before. There was no indication that he knew Zane was awake. Zane was about to whisper to him when he pivoted and headed into the bathroom.

Chapter Thirty-Two

"You should have turned this over as soon as you found it," FBI Agent Doug Oliphant said to Zane.

"You've got it now," Zane said.

The other agent, Melanie Strom, took the BlackBerry from her colleague and punched a few keys. "I miss this little keyboard," she said. "Best part of this phone."

The five of them sat in a grim little conference room in the FBI field office near 61st and Memorial. The agents looked different in the corporate setting under the flat fluorescent lights, more like bureaucrats and less like menacing law enforcement agents. The fact that Zane, Angel and Lettie had come here willingly, well, sort of, made today's meeting feel on more equal terms than the surprise invasion into the hotel room in North Hollywood.

Agent Oliphant was all business. "What did you find on it?"

"Nothing really," said Zane.

"Did you delete anything? Maybe something with your sister's information?"

"Why would I do that at this point?" Zane said. He figured the agent was just trying to wind him up. "Look, I'm relieved to be giving this to you. I'm in over my head here. I started out trying to help a friend then things got complicated. Now I'm just trying to protect my sister."

Zane shot a glance at Lettie, who sat next to him, her arm pressing slightly against his.

"How about you, Lettie? You do anything with this phone?"

"Not much to do with that phone. It barely supports text messages," she said. "I thought we were all friends here now."

"Enough, Lettie," Zane said.

"Thank you for bringing it to us," Strom said. "Remember they used to call these crackberries?" She gave a snorting laugh at the memory.

"So let's talk about how this is going to go down," Oliphant said. "Zane, you and Lettie are going to return the thumb drive to your contact Gene. You're going to give him a sob story about how you really need the money and how Lettie needs to keep working for them."

"Wait a minute—" Lettie said. She folded her arms across her chest, eyes on Oliphant.

"You all are changing the rules," Zane said. "I thought we returned this thumb drive and that's it, we're done. Because I'm not okay with her meeting him to do that." As he said it, Zane thought it sounded naïve. Had he really thought she wouldn't have had to direct in-person contact or had it been wishful thinking?

"I talked to our people and they said we need more from you. We need to really build a case here. There's a lot of pressure on us to log some wins here and you've gotten caught up in that."

"The goat pictures, huh?" Lettie said.

If there was the faintest smile around Strom's lips at Lettie's question, she erased it from her face in an instant. Zane had seen those photos on the FBI Twitter account: someone had hacked it a few weeks ago and posted goat face after goat face with really stupid meme jokes like "shit just goat real." Seemed like a harmless prank but he guessed if you were in charge of the FBI it was a bit embarrassing. But it wasn't fair that it changed what Lettie had to do and how long she had to be involved in this fiasco.

"She's just a kid," he said, "and you're putting her in harm's way because your bosses are embarrassed about a goat meme saying 'here we goat again?'"

"It's not about the goat pictures," Oliphant said. "It's about justice and doing the right thing. Fixing your mistakes and changing your trajectory." He aimed that last comment at Lettie like a bullet.

Zane stewed in the silence that followed his words, while Lettie and Oliphant stared each other down like dogs in a yard. Lettie broke eye contact first, after taking a sip of water from the bottle she'd brought with her. "Gives the word scapegoat new meaning," she grumbled.

"What was that?" Oliphant asked her irritably.

"Never mind," said Lettie. "Listen, I never knew who any of the big fish in this carding ring were. I got involved in it through Angel's mom. How am I going to get close to anyone now? They're not going to trust me."

"It's called a rock and a hard place, Lettie," Oliphant said. "You're a smart person. You're going to figure something out. Zane and Angel are going to help you."

Strom made a hushing gesture at Oliphant. "Look, the carding ring is one thing, but we're really after a hacker who goes by the name KellysEye. He—or she—has fingers in a lot of different money-making schemes. Your carding ring seems to be one of them. Malware that installs computer viruses that you have to pay him to get rid of, phishing schemes to trick businesses into paying fake invoices, that kind of thing. So that's the goal. But the first step is making contact with the group again, giving them back the USB drive, apologizing. Whatever you need to say."

"And we'd like you to make that call right now," Oliphant said.

"Make a call? That's not weird or anything," Lettie said. "I've never communicated with them that way before."

"So Signal or Telegram or WhatsApp them or however it is you reach them, and tell them you want your brother to meet with them to return the drive. Do it right here while we're watching," Oliphant said.

Lettie pulled her phone out of pocket. Oliphant and Strom moved their chairs around for a better look at her screen. Zane leaned over to look too:

I'm back in Tulsa and I want to give you back your property.

Zane managed to keep a brave face on for Lettie, but his nerves were jangling. He didn't relish the thought of another encounter with that man Gene or coming face-to-face with Kevin Perrine. He assumed that the people only got meaner and more dangerous as you traveled up the power hierarchy.

The response came fast.

Good move. When and where?

Lettie looked up. "Now what?"

"A public place is good and we can be ready this afternoon," Strom said. "How about the Gathering Place? Near the Skate Park?"

"What about the zoo?" Zane said. "I know that place better than anyone if things go wrong."

"Works for me," Strom said. Oliphant shrugged.

"Maybe at the children's zoo? That's where the baby goats are," Lettie said.

"Let it go, Lettie," Zane said. "By the elephants is good. It's always crowded and there's a janitorial building nearby if you all are going to be there."

Chapter Thirty-Three

It was one of those overcast but warm Tulsa spring days, green buds on bare grey-brown tree limbs scratching at an ominous and dark cloud bank north of downtown. At the zoo's front gate, Zane flashed the badge Gerry the facilities manager had neglected to take away from him before he left for Los Angeles.

The atmosphere was weekday afternoon slow. Two moms wheeling bright strollers chattered loudly like amp-ed up cockatoos. By the chimpanzee enclosure, every parent and kid with a smart phone wanted their own magic moment with the expressive primates for their social media feeds. Zane knew from experience that most of them would be lucky to snag a clear shot of one of the chimps. Between the bad lighting and wire fence and the animals' unpredictability, good photos were hard to come by. He sometimes wished people would just stop and enjoy the zoo experience instead of the endless photo-taking.

He'd arrived separately from the FBI agents but saw them parked in a car in the lot. Earlier, they had taped a wire to his chest so they could monitor what he said. They'd pitched it as protective but he knew it was also because they didn't trust him. And that was fine. He didn't trust them either. He didn't like the way this was shaping into some kind of one-way relationship with no end in sight for Lettie or for him. He needed to figure out a way to get them all out of this situation and then focus on how they would make their way forward with the new baby on the way.

Gerry, sleek as a sea lion, hoofed toward him belly-first. A plain brown baseball cap covered his bald head and shaded his eyes.

"And here you are," he called out.

Zane walked toward him and away from the central cluster of chimpanzee photographers.

"I told you I'd be back," Zane said.

"Left me in a bit of a pickle there, though," Gerry said.

"I know but my sister was in some trouble."

"Still is, I'm guessing," Gerry said, clipping his words as though he couldn't wait to be done with the conversation. "What made you come in today?"

Gerry's usual good-natured humor seemed to have vanished. Perhaps he was thinking too much about how Zane's father had killed the former facilities director and fed him to the Komodo dragon.

"I'm just meeting someone here, no big deal," Zane said.

"They said you were a troublemaker, but I saw a good kid who needed another chance," Gerry said. "But there's only so many chances."

"I hear you. I still need the job though, if it is still available."

Gerry's mustache twitched as he took a deep breath. He let it out slowly. "Well," he finally said, "I didn't hire anybody, so the position is still yours. For now. I'll put you back on the schedule starting tomorrow at seven o'clock if you want."

Zane's hopefulness returned. He had needed just one thing to break his way, and Gerry came through.

"Absolutely."

Zane's phone buzzed with a text message from Special Agent Strom.

Gene's here.

"I've got to go," Zane said.

"I'll keep my eye on you," Gerry said. Zane could tell he meant it in a protective way even without the clap on the back the man delivered before he headed toward the chimpanzees.

From the big enclosure where the elephants lived, Zane heard one giving a bleating trumpet. Normally he thought of it as a playful, excited sound, but today it set his teeth on edge. It felt like a warning.

As if on cue, Gene appeared. Surly, watchful and muscle-bound, he didn't belong in the happy, family-friendly environment. Zane noticed a toddler in a stroller pointing at him as he walked by, probably entranced by the porcupine hair.

"I had to pay to get in this stupid place," Gene said by way of greeting. "I thought it was free."

"You've never been here before?"

"Are you kidding me?"

"I thought most people came here for an elementary school field trip or something, at least," Zane said.

Gene seemed amused by his nervous chatter. "I didn't grow up in this shithole town," he said.

"Right, you just chose it as an adult," Zane said.

Gene's eyes narrowed as he took Zane's measure. Then he gave a half-laugh. "Yeah, I guess so."

The largest elephant, Bruno, lumbered over to the feeding station and grasped a hunk of grass with his trunk. They watched as she curled it gracefully into his mouth and chewed.

"How much do those things weigh?"

"I dunno, like five tons or something? More than a car."

"They must have to eat all the goddamned day," Gene said. "So where's your sister?"

Zane studied his face. If the man meant the comment to be some sort of stupid fat joke about Lettie's size, he didn't show any signs of it. Zane let it slide.

"I've got the thumb drive. She's not coming." He reached into his jeans pocket and pulled out the source of all this trouble.

Gene sucked in his breath with a sniff. "Everything's still on it?"

"Yeah."

"Hand it over, then."

Zane dropped it into his outstretched palm, noticing the black tattoo on the inside of his arm reading "Regret Nothing." On most people, Zane thought the words might be read as inspirational or hopeful. On this sociopath, it came off as frightening. He probably did regret nothing, which made him a dangerous foe. Zane felt the fear settle in his stomach like a bag of rocks. He wanted nothing more than to get away from him. But he had one more thing to do.

"So... Lettie's a good kid," he started, faltering a bit.

Gene ground his jaw. "If you say so."

"Look, I mean, what I'm trying to say—"

"I'm not going to say she's out of trouble here with us. I gotta take this back, make sure everything's still on it."

"That's not it. What it is, well, we need the money—"

"You got some nerve, I'll give you that," Gene said. "We're not paying you for our property."

"Can't Lettie still work for you?" Zane finally blurted out.

Gene grunted and let his mouth hang open slightly. His eyes scanned the horizon in quick mechanical flicks, reminding Zane of the Terminator from those movies.

He turned his gaze back to Zane. "I didn't expect you to say that."

Zane repeated that they needed the money and added in what he hoped were convincing reassurances that she wouldn't take anything from them again. He forced himself to keep eye contact, or at least look like he was, by staring at the place where the man's dark eyebrows merged into one over his nose.

"I'll pass it on," Gene said.

"To who? Is there someone I should talk to besides you?"

"Not yet," Gene said. He pocketed the thumb drive and stomped back toward the entrance.

Adrenalin still spiking through his nervous system, Zane forced himself to walk instead of run across the plaza to the parking lot where Agents Strom and Oliphant sat. That dark cloud bank that was threatening downtown when Zane arrived had moved over the zoo, blocking out the sun. A cold gust of wind chilled his sweat-damp skin and shirt.

April in Tulsa was a wet, violent month, the middle in a string of three filled with wind and water and short spells of sunshine called tornado season. A tornado was all the stress he needed right now..

Sure enough, just as he watched Gene peel out of the parking lot in a Dodge Challenger, his cell phone alarm an emergency alert from the weather service. He reached for his phone to read the message.

"Funnel cloud spotted in Sand Springs," the message said. He shrugged it off with a dose of fatalism. If it was his time, it was his time, he thought. Sand Springs was about fifteen miles from the zoo.

He slid into the back seat of the FBI agents' car. "Is there a tornado shelter we should go into?" Oliphant said. His eyes scanned the dark cloud bank.

Zane couldn't stop the small chuckle from bursting forth.

"Excuse me?" Oliphant swiveled and glared at him.

"You're not from around here, are you?" Zane said. "We don't get into the tornado shelter until we see that cloud coming straight for us."

The verbal flex was a useless bit of macho bravado but it still made Zane smile to see Oliphant squirm a bit. He didn't like the guy much.

"You probably have so many of these this time of year, you get kind of casual about them," Strom said. But Oliphant continued to seethe. He kept his eyes trained on Zane with a nasty glare, like a kangaroo preparing to deliver a punch. Zane watched as the agent's ears grew red. The guy definitely had some kind of anger management problem.

"You did all right out there, Zane," Strom said. "How are you feeling?" And then she reached out and touched Oliphant's arm. It was a small, subtle gesture, but it seemed to calm him a bit. Her words had the same kind of calming effect on Zane. Wisps of hair had escaped her ponytail and gone puffy from the dampening air, creating a soft halo around her face, not unlike a koala bear's fur.

"I wish that was the last time I had to see that guy," Zane said. "What if they don't take Lettie back?" This was his hope. Surely these criminals weren't dumb enough to take someone who had stolen from them back into the fold.

"Don't try to sabotage this, Zane. We'll know."

"Okay, I get it," Zane said. But getting it didn't mean he had taken it to heart. If he could figure a way out of this hell, he would do it. Anything to protect Lettie and get her as far from these criminals as possible.

"What you don't realize, Zane, is that criminals work with

people they don't trust all the time. They're used to it. So I wouldn't be surprised if they give her the job back," Strom said.

Zane wondered if that was meant to be reassuring.

"What's the bottom line here? What would be the ideal thing Lettie found for you?"

Oliphant decided to turn his punchy anger on Zane again. He leaned backwards so close that Zane could smell his coffee breath. "We need access to the exit and entry points. That's the only way we can make a case."

"Exit and entry points?"

"He means the devices used to initiate criminal activity, you know," Strom said. "The computers or phones they're using to hack into systems or sell items on the dark web."

"What about the BlackBerry? Did that have anything on it?"

The agents exchanged glances. "We're still working on it," Strom said.

"What if that's the key?"

"I doubt you'll get that lucky," Oliphant said.

Zane felt a pit of dread opening up in his stomach, like a big black hole he was slowly falling through. He shoved his hands in his pockets to hide the twinges of trembling in his fingers.

"Look, all we can do is follow breadcrumbs until we can make a case," Strom said. "Sometimes you never know where the smallest things will lead."

Zane must have looked crestfallen because Strom reached out and gave him the same kind of cheery arm pat she'd delivered to Oliphant a few minutes earlier.

"Have faith," she said.

Chapter Thirty-Four

Zane drove straight to Ernest Buckskin's for a sweat when he left the zoo. On the way, he called Verda to check in on Lettie and Angel. All was well and calm, for the moment at least. He was glad to be rid of the thumb drive and could hear the relief in Lettie's voice too when he told her. He could also tell that she was holding on to the same hope he was. Maybe they wouldn't take her back. Maybe she had burned their trust. There wasn't any reason to fill Lettie in on Strom's statement about criminals working with people they didn't trust all the time.

On the compound, all was quiet. The brown tabby cat and a few chickens followed him as he walked toward the house. The cat pounced on black beetle in a clump of green grass, pawing it with her claw before chomping her mouth down on it. The chickens lagged behind, poking and dancing their beaks at the dirt. Puddles full of red muddy water spotted the land from the rain.

He heard his name and turned toward the shade of willows growing on the north side of the house. Ernest sat with his legs straight out in front of him, his back curved like the willow branch above him. The cat slunk beside his outstretched legs and Ernest ran his fingers down her back. Zane could hear the purr from ten feet away. The shadows of the willow leaves made Ernest's skin look mottled and dark, like scales of a fish.

Zane squatted in the dirt beside him, feeling the sunlight move up and down his body like hands. The muscles of his neck and shoulders relaxed and he closed his eyes for a moment. Except for the sound of the cat's purr and chickens' scratch, it was quiet.

When he opened his eyes again, Ernest spoke. "You look tired," he said. "Do you want to eat?"

He didn't. He'd indulged in a fried chicken sandwich and fries in the car. The greasy meal still felt like glue on his insides.

"What is going on with Lettie?"

"How do you know it's about Lettie?"

"I don't know, just a hunch," he said.

"She is helping this criminal ring steal people's credit card numbers."

"I'm sorry to hear that."

Zane looked off into the distance, toward the low hills in the south. "It's gotten complicated."

Ernest rose to his feet, shaking dust off of his hands when he was upright.

"Come on, then," he said. "Let's do a sweat." They walked around the side of the house toward the sweat lodge. Sun-faded tarps hung from bent poles over the sweat lodge in the back.

"Is Dirk here?" Ernest shook his head.

"Just us today. Well, you and your demons," Ernest said.

"The way my mom left my dad, hid me from him, when I was a kid. It must have messed me up," Zane said. "The way I was raised, maybe."

"Everything's more complicated than you think," Ernest said. "There's no one thing."

But Zane wished there were. What if there was that one thing that happened to you that could be erased? Memories of trauma and loss evaporated. Who would you be without that tragedy? How would your life change?

Once the rocks were heated up and carried with a pitchfork into the sweat lodge, Zane and Ernest changed into baggy shorts. Ernest pulled the tarp down and sealed them inside. Zane scattered powdered leaves and herbs onto the hot stones. When the pungent smell of burning tobacco, hemlock, sage and cedar bark rose into the air, he ladled scoops of water onto the rocks. Hot steam coated his lungs. They prayed.

After some time, Ernest threw the tarp aside and left to get more rocks from the fire. He ladled more water onto them and steam filled the space. Zane felt dizzy and lay down, rough towel across his face. His stomach rumbled and rolled over the food he had eaten on the drive. This was why it was important to fast before a sweat, he thought. He felt queasy but tried to concentrate on Ernest chanting a long prayer to the immortals and to the departed ancestors. Then Ernest said it was time for him to speak and all Zane could think to say was "I'm failing to protect Lettie."

Ernest paused for a few beats, thinking.

"You are doing your best," he said finally. "Remember what I told you before? People on this earth have fought terrible battles and overcome tremendous challenges. They have fought monsters and won with the kinds of spiritual practices I talk about here. I'm not talking about the magic you see in the movies where a man or woman waves a wand. I'm talking about this deep truth we can find in this place for healing. This kind of magic is beyond what most understand today. Almost lost."

"I wish my mother was here," Zane said. "She'd know what to do with Lettie."

"Your mother is with you all the time," Ernest said. "But she was a human mother. She didn't always know what to do. She knew to do her best but she was as confused as you. She was a regular person just like you're a regular person. She'd lived longer so she had more life experiences than you. But you're smart. You know this."

"I still feel like a kid. I don't know how to adult."

"Quit saying dumb things. Let me ask you a question. What is Lettie's greatest strength?"

Zane finally answered.

"She's smart. Like really smart. Smarter than me. You should see her on the computer stuff."

"What else?"

"She's determined. What's that word for when you keep moving forward despite obstacles? Resilience. She has this drive to keep going. Doesn't fall into depression like me."

"What else?"

"She likes to draw. She used to create these crazy complicated drawings of fairies and elves. I'd be amazed at how detailed they were. They could have been in some picture book."

Zane was crying now. Ernest sat quietly while Zane let the feelings wash over him: fear, sadness, regret, frustration.

"Now don't you cry for yourself any longer. We don't get to choose what happens to us in this life. We choose how we react to it. You haven't had an easy life. Neither has Lettie. But you put all that energy into making things as smooth as you can for her. She's young and her life is only now shaping up. You put all that energy into finding a way out of this current mess. Have you been drinking again?"

"No."

"Good."

Ernest left the lodge again and returned balancing more rocks on his pitchfork. He laid them in the center. He drew another two ladles of water from the barrel and poured them on the stones, steaming rising again as Zane cried his last tears for himself.

Being steamed like a fish for supper cleared his mind but not his worry. Still, he slept like the dead that night, dreamless and flat on his back with hands crossed on his chest. He woke up in the same position, his neck stiff. He pictured his worry as a clump of ice. It lay so heavy and cold in his stomach that he could feel it, numbing the energy out of him. The only path forward was to take one step. The old Alcoholics Anonymous adages held truth for lots of situations, not just drinking. One day at a time. And today he had to work at the zoo.

Zane arrived at the zoo and clocked in just as Chris arrived. Nobody would ever call Chris a sensitive person but Zane saw concern stitched onto his face as their eyes met. Maybe also some wariness and certainly curiosity. People got funny when law-and-order types started hanging around, Zane knew from experience.

Gerry had written work assignments on the white board in a black scrawl. The zoo owned an industrial floor waxer and the reptile pavilion needed Zane's attention. Chris's assignment was to clear leaves from the entrance with the air blower.

"Need some help with that?" Chris asked. Zane's eyebrows shot up in surprise. Chris had never offered to help him before.

"I'm good."

Over at the reptile pavilion, he moved the map stands and

the doormats outside. He swept the floor with the broom, trying to still his mind. Soft light glowed from the glass-fronted pens sunk flush into the walls on either side of him. They resembled a series of television screens tuned to different but similar channels, floodlit landscapes, camouflaged snakes. Montages of rock and branch, and scattered leaves and wood chips dry as crackers in which little activity was visible.

After the wax was on the floor, he turned on the buffer and began. The machine hummed and vibrated. He moved it back and forth. The sound was low and mesmerizing. The reptile specialist had told him how funny it was that people spoke in hushed tones around snakes, not realizing they were deaf. All snakes can detect are ground-borne vibrations, which is why the mechanical buffer was causing a bit of a stir in the pens. The Indian cobra began rubbing its head against a branch, forcing a tear in its skin that would start the process of shedding. It inched itself through the process with a steady series of tiny shrugs. Zane finished the waxing and returned to the pen, where the cobra's old skin had begun peeling away, trailing from the snake dried and crumbly but intact, to reveal a skin beneath that shined more than the floor Zane had just waxed.

The animals at the zoo often had the capacity to surprise him, and for this reason exactly, the snakes were his favorites. It alone of all the creatures seemed the most able to renew itself, undoubtedly why the *ouroboros*—a circular symbol depicting a snake eating its own tail—represented the eternal cycle of destruction and rebirth. He watched in silence while the snake stripped itself of its old skin and returned to a new beginning. It seemed like magic, the kind he had hoped for in the sweat lodge with Ernest but was not yet sure he had found.

The trill of the video chat app on his smartphone jolted him out of his reverie. It was Maxine. Her face filled the phone's narrow screen and Zane raised his arm so his own phone's camera wasn't shooting straight up his nostrils.

The glow of the cell phone screen was bright in the dim room but the snakes did not seem to notice.

"Hey! How are you doing?" Maxine said. Her high energy bounced off the screen.

"I've been better," Zane answered honestly.

Maxine raked her fingers through her hair. "We hadn't talked in a while. I heard from Tiffany that Lettie went missing but you have her back home now. That must have been scary."

It was but Zane resisted the temptation to spill his guts about it to her. He was in deep enough shit to know to keep his mouth shut about things. Besides, it sounded like Tiffany was sharing enough.

"Definitely. So what's up? I'm in the middle of work."

"Yeah, right. So where is Lettie? I tried calling her to see if she wanted to talk through anything but she didn't pick up."

Zane's antenna for danger rose. Suddenly, he had a queasy feeling in his stomach. Sure, Maxine had been helpful and Lettie seemed to have a friendship with her, but what did he really know about her? Could he trust her? Could he trust Tiffany as much as he already had? Damn, he could be stupid when it came to attractive women.

"I'll tell her you're trying to reach her, okay?" Zane dodged the question like a boxer ducking from a jab.

"I just thought maybe I could bring her some stones to help with her energy," Maxine said.

"I'll let her know," Zane said. "I've gotta go." He hit the screen's red button to end the call before she asked again. He didn't feel good shutting down her request but he also thought it was the right thing to do.

The phone trilled again and Old Spice's name filled the screen this time.

"Zane, where are you?"

"At work, why?"

"You might want to come home if you can," the detective said.

"What for?"

"Kevin Perrine is dead."

A dozen heartbeats full of relief pumped away the queasy feeling talking to Maxine had given him. Not that he had wished for the man's death, but without a doubt, there was comfort in knowing he was out of the picture and couldn't hurt Lettie.

"Dead?"

"Not just dead, but dead in his car in your apartment's parking lot," Old Spice said.

"When? When did he die?"

"Not sure yet," the detective said. "Looks kind of recent. Where have you been?"

Zane realized he was holding his breath. "Work," he said. "Since six-thirty." The phone's clock in the upper righthand corner read three minutes after eight. What a shitshow of a day and it wasn't even mid-morning yet.

"Can you leave work and come home?"

Gerry wasn't going to like this at all.

"Let me see what I can do," Zane said. At least he had buffed the floor. Maybe Gerry would cut him some slack for that.

Chapter Thirty-Five

The parking lot of Zane's apartment complex in east Tulsa was full of police cars. Zane parked outside his building, one of eight identical apartment buildings on the weedy but mowed lot off of Memorial. He texted Old Spice that he had arrived but he didn't need to. He was there, on site, talking to a woman. They both turned and waved at Zane. It was Agent Strom.

A white pop-up tent sat beside a dirty white Toyota Prius, and inside the car, Zane caught a glimpse of a body slumped in the front seat in an unnatural position. Two photographers—one in a Tulsa Police Department jacket, the other in the FBI's version—moved around the scene like boxers in the ring. The police and the photographers had an unprofessional air of amusement brought out by the fact that Perrine's pants were unfastened and unzipped, a pair of tighty-whiteys showing. A secondary point of curiosity was the copy of Oprah Magazine open on the seat next to him.

Meanwhile the media had been sequestered on the other side of the parking lot, where he could see the van from KTUL-

TV. Kristy Diguchi, the reporter who had chased him all over the Majestic Trailer Park after his mother died, stood talking to a cameraman. She caught Zane's eye and waved frantically but he ignored her.

Old Spice and Strom stood apart from the central crowd of onlookers, both in sunglasses. Zane joined them.

"How long has he been there?" Zane asked them.

"Maybe a few hours. Did you see the car when you left this morning?"

Zane racked his brain trying to recreate the morning. He couldn't recall seeing the Prius, but there were so many of those cars around he wasn't sure he would have noticed. If Perrine had been in the brown Subaru he saw at Bamboozles, he would have noticed that. It came to him: this felt just like the days after his mother's death. Arno Jackson's body had been found in the woods behind the Majestic not long after Zane's mother was killed, and for a time, Zane was suspect number one. This had to be a curse, he thought. Maybe Lettie was on to something with her protective spells. This world was off-balance, dangerous, unfair.

Zane said he didn't remember seeing it and asked if he could take a closer look at the body. Strom asked why.

"Because he's been chasing me and my sister for a week now. I need closure."

Old Spice said, "You're taking this very personally."

"Wouldn't you?" Zane snapped.

"It's understandable," Strom said to Old Spice. "However you might want to know that Mr. Perrine lost control of his bowels when he died. The smell is a little hard to take."

"It can't smell worse than the zoo bathroom on a hot day and a trash can full of dirty diapers," Zane said.

"Don't touch anything," Old Spice said as he walked Zane over to the car.

Kevin Perrine was dead all right—Zane wasn't sure why he needed to confirm this up close but seeing his body did have an effect on his anxiety. It heightened it. Perrine wasn't chasing them anymore. Someone else—someone worse?—had executed him with a bullet to the head. Zane held his breath and looked at the man's face. Except for the strange angle of the neck and the gunshot wound, he could have been asleep. His eyes were shut and his right hand rested on the magazine, open to a story about feeling sexy after age fifty.

A uniformed officer rushed up to Old Spice and asked to talk for a minute. The two moved out of earshot for the conversation. Strom took advantage of the moment alone and surprised Zane by reaching around his shoulders for a partial hug. Zane was surprised again at how comforting it felt.

"It's been a lot for you," she said with a warm look of concern.

He nodded as they pulled apart. Having her acknowledge that meant something to him, even if she was partly responsible for the stress he was under. Scratch that. His stress and anxiety was really about Lettie and his failure as her guardian. He should have paid more attention to what she was doing.

"Do you have kids?"

Strom shook her head.

"I never realized how hard it was to be a parent until I became Lettie's guardian. I owe my mom some serious apologies."

"Don't we all," Strom said.

Two men with CORONER'S OFFICE written on their jackets wheeled a stretcher to the car and studied it and Perrine for a moment as though making a plan. A woman trailed behind them with a blue tarp.

When Old Spice returned, he was excited. "God how I

love that everyone has one of those camera doorbells these days," he said.

"What did you find?" asked Strom.

"Got the killer on video. Easy peasy."

"Unbelievable."

"You mean...I'm in the clear?"

"Looks like it, Zane," Old Spice said.

"But who is it?"

"Can't quite make out the face because of a hoodie but we've got a license plate of the car he came out of. It's just a matter of time."

"I don't like how things are escalating," Strom said.

Zane didn't either.

Chapter Thirty-Six

Lettie's reaction to Kevin Perrine's death was more frightened than relieved too.

"We had just been doing some tarot card readings and—"

"Lettie, I only need good news at this point."

She held up a card to her phone's camera. A drawing of a castle turret with two figures falling from it appeared on his phone's screen. At the bottom, it read THE TOWER.

"So that looks like destruction," Zane said. He really didn't need a deck of cards telling him how bad things were.

"Did you see that movie Lord of the Rings?" Angel asked from somewhere off camera. "It's all about an epic battle to end evil by destroying the dark tower."

"I've seen the movie," Zane said. "This isn't a movie. This is our lives."

"The Tower card is about shattering a long-standing situation. Upheaval, conflict. This isn't any surprise, Zane. This is what we know. But there's hope in this. A liberation," Lettie said.

"I certainly hope so."

"Guess what turned up in the future position? Three of wands." She held up a card showing a man standing on a hilltop watching boats sail beneath him.

"It's a strong card. It represents a position of power. We're going to get through this, Zane," she said. Zane heard the ping of a text alert. He saw her scroll to and read the words, and then her brave performance faltered a bit.

"I just got a text from Gene," she said.

A metallic taste came into Zane's mouth. "What does it say?"

Lettie kept staring at the screen, as though trying to digest the words fully. Zane realized she was even more scared than he had thought. "He wants to know if I'll clean some files. Says he's going to send me the link. I guess I'm back in their employ," she said.

Zane tried to keep his own fear under control. The effort this took brought him close to tears, but when he spoke, he did his best to sound businesslike, as though this were a job at Braum's Ice Cream instead of an identity theft ring. "What does that mean to clean some files? Do you have to meet him?"

"No, I mean, he doesn't say that. It's scrum work really, just checking batches of card numbers to make sure they work. You put small charges on them," she said. It sounded harmless enough and if she didn't have to meet Gene or any of his criminal friends, that much the better.

"Okay, I'll let Agent Strom know then," Zane said. "You're back in business."

The phone trilled again as he drove back to the zoo.

"You coming back to work again?" Bingo Pratt's voice crackled through a bad connection.

"Hey Bingo. Yeah, I was going to call you," Zane lied. He hadn't even thought about talking to Bingo. He'd figured the carnival was leaving soon enough, and he didn't feel like groveling for another job. Begging for the zoo job was bad enough. Still, he could use the money, and who knew how Gerry was going to react to this time off today.

"Even if you don't want to come back to work, we want you to come to the closing night party. Everyone cuts loose, we bring in a keg, have a few laughs. We'd love to have you there."

Bingo's friendly tone caught him off-guard but he welcomed it.

"I could work a couple of shifts before you close if you still need the help. And the closing night party sounds fun. Can I bring someone?"

"Lettie's invited, of course," Bingo said. "It's family friendly, I promise."

"Oh, right," Zane laughed. "I meant someone else. A woman."

"Sure, bring a date. The more the merrier we always say. Someone special?"

"I think so but that's what I'm trying to figure out. Hey, listen, you ought to know that the police found that guy Kevin Perrine dead today."

"The guy who knifed the other guy?"

"He was found shot in the parking lot of my apartment complex."

Bingo paused for so long Zane thought the cell connection was lost. He was just about to start doing the "can you hear me now?" thing when the man finally spoke.

"You sure are a magnet for trouble, aren't you?"

Zane didn't like his tone. "You're making a mistake if you think I'm at the center of these things. I'm a case of wrong place, wrong time, here."

"Worst luck I've ever heard of."

"I don't intend to bring any more trouble to the carnival if that's what you mean."

"Shit, Zane, I don't care about it. I've just never met anyone with such bad fortune before. The business with your dad, this stuff, Lettie going missing. Where is she?"

"She's safe now," Zane said. "I've got to go, so can we talk later?"

"One last question," Bingo said.

"Okay."

"Do you have a gun?"

The question surprised Zane so much that he doubted he'd heard the question right.

"A gun? I do not," he said. "Why? Do you need one?"

"No, I was just curious. Some of the security guys we hire carry them, that's all. I wondered if you did."

Zane didn't remember any questions like that during Bingo's casual job interview process. But he let it drop. There was only so much energy he could put toward worrying about what Bingo meant by something. He turned onto the Mohawk Park entrance road, a big dark-windowed truck right on his bumper. When it honked, he looked in the rearview mirror and gave a wave. The park road was too narrow to pass so he sped up a bit.

"I gotta clock in at the zoo," he said, ending the call and tossing the phone onto the passenger seat. Long and lined with trees, the drive was a straight shot to the main parking lot. Most of the trees strung along the road sprouted tender green leaves thanks to the spring rain. The truck honked again, then sped up behind him, swept out half onto the grass and around him to zoom through the park entrance kiosk and make a left on Cherokee Drive. He fought the urge to chase the truck and pick a fight, slowing his breath to try to slow his pulse. It was hard being a guardian and a brother; he was no better at it today than he was when he started. He just kept trying. He turned the notion over in his head like the worry stone he used to carry in his pocket, examining its crevices and bulges for some insight. If only his mother had lived. If only Lettie's father wasn't in prison. If only he had seen the signs of Lettie's dip into criminality earlier. He had to get Lettie clear of this. He had to find a way.

Chapter Thirty-Seven

Lettie called again while Zane was emptying trash cans by the elephant habitat. Within seconds of picking up, another call beeped in. It was Lettie's school. Zane hit the ignore-call button.

"Your school wants to know when you're coming back," he said. "I'm not sure what to tell them."

"I was thinking about that. Why can't we come back to Tulsa? It makes more sense than being out in the sticks with Verda. Her Internet is terrible."

"I really need some positivity here," Zane said.

"The only way through this is directly into the fire," she said. "How am I supposed to get them to tell me where the servers are located? And that's the only way out. Those FBI agents basically said so."

She had a point.

"Verda even said she'd drive us to Tulsa," Lettie said. She lowered her voice to a whisper. "She says we need to be back in school but I think she's terrified we're going to have sex in the house."

"Okay, come home then. Have her bring you tonight. But call those agents and tell them what the plan is. And I'll call your school."

"One more thing," she said.

"Yeah?"

"I think I need to see a doctor. Maybe get some pre-natal vitamins, that kind of thing."

"Of course. See if you can make an appointment at that clinic by the apartment. That's a great idea. And you know there's one more call to make. We need to tell Gene you're coming back. But I'll do it."

Zane tossed the full trash bag onto the golf cart and put in a fresh liner. From the cart, he called Gene. He didn't pick up, so Zane left a message saying that Lettie was coming back to Tulsa and he expected that she would be safe. Then he made one more call.

"Hey," Tiffany said.

"How's Tulsa's best phone fixer?"

"At work. It's slow."

"This is going to sound sort of sudden, and you can say no, but is there any way you could meet me for a coffee or dinner or something tonight? I'd really like to see you."

"Sure, I can meet you at Scooter's Coffee on my break at seven."

A relieved smile rose to Zane's face.

"Perfect."

"Do I need to bring anything? Like old BlackBerry chargers or a dial-up modem or something?"

"No old technology needed. And let me buy you the coffee too."

"Be warned. I like the real expensive ones with syrups and whipped cream," she said.

"I've got you."

. . .

It was clear that Tiffany was not thrilled to see Lettie sitting at the table with Zane when she entered the coffee shop. It was, after all, their first date. However, Angel had gone home to check in on his mom and Lettie was creeped out by the crime scene tape in the parking lot where Kevin Perrine had died, so he had to bring her along. He didn't mind keeping a closer eye on her than usual, even if it cramped his love life a bit.

"How was Los Angeles?" She asked Lettie, drawing out the city name so it sounded like *Law-ss Ain-gee-less* and Zane was charmed all over again. He was a sucker for a woman with a country accent.

"It was different than I thought it would be," Lettie said. "Grittier and also more fake than I expected. Did you know the palm trees were imported? They don't grow naturally there."

"I didn't know that," Tiffany said. The *dint* instead of didn't again.

"Still, I met a few cool people," Lettie said.

The coffee shop was empty but for one guy with a laptop and big headphones on, video of a dog running visible on his screen. Ambient electronica music floated through the air. One by one they ordered their coffee drinks from the barista, who wore the regulation jeans/novelty T-shirt/blue hair/white apron of the coffee worker set. True to her word, Tiffany ordered a ridiculously complicated drink: five shots of espresso over ice, four pumps of vanilla with extra oat milk, add caramel drizzle and a dash of cinnamon.

Zane ordered an iced tea and eyed the picked-over set of sad sandwiches in the refrigerated case. What made him suggest coffee? He could really use a real meal and there was a Cracker Barrel just around the corner. He grabbed the least-sad ham-and-cheese sandwich and gestured for Lettie to do the same. She just shook her head. "Not hungry. We ate on the way back from Verda's."

"Did you hear about that guy who knifed my stepmom's friend?" Tiffany said. "The police found him dead in some apartment parking lot."

"We heard all right," Lettie said. She slung her backpack onto a chair and plopped down next to it.

"He was found dead in our apartment building parking lot, actually," Zane said.

"Are you kidding?"

"Not at all."

Tiffany mulled the news, pushing her phone around on the table as Lettie pulled out an Oklahoma history textbook with a sigh.

"What do you think is going on?" she finally asked. There was something about the way she looked up, the way her eyes shone, that made Zane think of the nursery rhyme his mother had sometimes sung to him when he was five or six: *Yet if thy blue eyes I see, gloom will soon depart. For to me, sweet Aura Lee, is sunshine to the heart.* Tiffany's eyes were brown, not blue, but the detail didn't matter. The emotion was the same. Even as she asked him about the murder that was top of his mind, he still felt calmer to be with her.

A quick glance at Lettie's raised eyebrows and amused smile let him know he had been staring at Tiffany a few beats too long.

"I think—really I hope—that this is the end of it. Wally Zittman's killer is dead," Zane said.

"Maxine says it doesn't add up," Tiffany said. "It makes her think that there is way more to the story than we've seen."

"Does she know something specific?" Zane felt intensely thirsty and glanced at the counter where the barista stood behind a hissing espresso machine. The problem with crime and subterfuge and lying was that Zane felt like he was performing all the time now, on guard against authenticity in favor of projecting confidence or whatever it was he was supposed to be projecting to help Lettie get through this and onto the world of studies and college and a better life. He wished he could confide in Tiffany, but he was smart enough to realize that he just didn't know her well enough to trust her, no matter how much he would like to.

"Just her intuition, really," Tiffany said. "Maxine just was asking why someone would want both men dead. And also pointing out that it meant another killer was at large."

Lettie stared at her Oklahoma history textbook as though it was a map back to their old life, before the credit card ring and the FBI. He wished it were.

"Anyway, you won't believe who came into the store earlier today," Tiffany said. "Your boss from the carnival, whathisname?"

"Bingo Pratt?"

"No, I would have remembered that. The guy who came up to you and asked you to do something the night I came by? That first night we met?" Tiffany gave him a bright smile that brought a matching one to his, even though he didn't like the coincidence.

"Do you mean Mike? Short guy, looks like he swallowed a yoga ball?"

"Yeah, that's him. He came in to get a cracked screen fixed. He mentioned there was this closing night party."

"Oh, yeah, I just heard about that."

"Party?" Lettie looked up with mild interest.

"Closing night kegger before they leave town," Zane said. "I was thinking about going."

"Maybe we could make it a date," Tiffany said before Zane had found the words and the nerve to ask her the same thing.

"Absolutely," Zane said. "I wasn't sure you'd want to go."

"Your life is like this unfolding story. I'm interested to see what happens next," Tiffany said.

"All right lovebirds, now that we've got that sorted, can one of you help me get the drinks?" Lettie said, rolling her eyes.

Chapter Thirty-Eight

The mood of the carnival on its last night was high, hip-hop music blasting against the thunderous sounds of the rides and diesel generators, bright lights still shimmering, punctuated with brassy laughter. Pointing, smiling, chattering people surged down the midway and to the rides like water overflowing gutters. Bingo was in a great mood, walking through the crowd, watching tickets and dollars changing hands. It seemed like everyone from the woman who sold caramel-dipped apples to the guy who operated the Tilt-a-Whirl to the truck drivers was in a jovial mood too, ready to shake off Tulsa like a duck shakes off water and move on to the promise of new places and new pockets filled with money.

Zane picked at Lettie's cheesy nachos when he saw a head of blond spiked hair making its way through the crowd. Sure enough, the crowd parted and Gene emerged into the food area, his arm clamped around a tinselly dancer-type wearing a shredded T-shirt and tight jeans. Zane assumed she was one of his employees at Bamboozles.

"Hey, it's Kayleigh!" Angel said, waving at the woman. "You remember her, don't you, Zane?"

"She looks different without the pink wig," Zane said.

"I bet she looks different with clothes on too," Lettie said.

Kayleigh gave them all a big high-cheeked smile as the couple approached the table. She looked tiny and breakable next to Gene's heavy bulldog body. Up close, she also looked like a teenager, underneath the cat-eye and bright pink lips.

"If it isn't my prodigal employee, Lettie," Gene said. "With her posse."

Gene's tone had an edge Zane didn't care for. He took a breath, thinking how much he would enjoy seeing this man locked away for good. Lettie was unfazed.

"You know you're glad to have me back," she said. She scraped up melted cheese with a broken tortilla chip.

Gene paused, taking their measure like a teacher deciding how to discipline an unruly but favorite child. His short laugh sounded mocking. "You always were as tough as nails for a kid," he said to Lettie. "You two losers have to watch out for her. She'll run your show."

"I don't mind that," Angel said. "She's smarter than me." He leaned into Lettie in a way that looked partly like reassurance and partly like protection.

Zane made himself laugh too. He wanted to look relaxed. "She's definitely the brains in the family."

From yards away, he saw Tiffany standing in the crowd. She swiped at her phone, probably texting him, but he watched her instead of checking his phone or waving. He wanted to tell her to go the other way. He didn't want Gene to know her or even see her. She waited a few beats, swiping at the phone fast as though dismissing bad thoughts. She looked determined and smart, he thought, scanning the crowd until her eyes found his at the table. A smile grew on her face, a joy to watch, as she came closer.

"Who do we have here?" Gene said. He practically licked his lips at Tiffany, giving her a gross once-over like she was a stripper coming to audition. She returned the stare with raised eyebrows and a fake smile.

Zane did the introductions but made a fuss about having to get Tiffany some food as a way to shake Gene. He didn't look likely to take the hint, but Kayleigh came through instead, saying that he had promised her a ride on the Ferris wheel before it closed for good and could they go now.

"So what is Gene doing here?" Zane asked.

"I don't know but my mom and him go way back. Maybe she invited him," Angel said.

Zane looked at Lettie, wondering if they should have told the FBI agents they were coming to the carnival tonight. She must have had the same question cross her mind, because she returned the look with a little shrug.

A knot of people stood around a small pop-up tent Zane hadn't seen before on the carnival row. Purple duct tape affixed a sign that said "Palm Readings $5" to its top.

"Does your stepmom got a side hustle going?"

"I hadn't heard," Tiffany said, walking toward the tent to take a peek.

One of palm reading bystanders, an attractive woman in a hoodie and cargo pants, spotted Zane and Lettie and began walking toward them. Her long, brown hair was pulled into a neat ponytail with a part as straight as a laser beam and big, black-framed glasses. Zane didn't recognize her until she got close.

"Hey, what's up?"

"What are you doing here?"

"Beautiful spring night. Who doesn't love a carnival?"

"Bullshit," Lettie said. "We were just saying we should have told you about this."

Agent Strom laughed. "We have our ways."

Her laugh was guileless enough that Zane felt comfortable that she didn't think they were keeping anything from the FBI. They didn't need that kind of headache.

"Where's your partner?"

"Around."

They moved to a place where they could talk, near one of the buzzing portable light towers Bingo had set up on the perimeter. A couple empty beer bottles sat on top the orange generator like a bar. "There are a lot of interesting characters here tonight," she said. "And yes, you should keep us apprised of what you're doing. Tonight just keep it real and see what you can find out. Do you feel like they trust you, Lettie?"

"Not sure."

"Yeah," Strom nodded. "It hasn't been that long. Just keep your eyes and ears open."

"Is the carnival somehow related to the identity theft ring?" Zane asked.

Strom motioned around the grounds with her hand and said, "There's definitely some illegal stuff going on here. But you already know that. Just pay attention and let me know if you hear anything." She walked off carrying the two empty beer bottles in her hand, passing a curious Tiffany on her way to the trash can.

"Who was that? Litter patrol?" Tiffany said. "I was looking for you guys and you disappeared."

"One of my mom's friends," Angel said.

"Your mom hangs out with cops?" Tiffany replied.

"What makes you think she's a cop? My mom knows lots of different kinds of people," Angel said.

"Gee, I don't know, the gun under her shirt?" Tiffany said.

By eleven o'clock, it had turned into a weird night. Most of the families with kids had left and those who stayed were a motley mix of carnival workers, strippers from Bamboozles, and tweakers and thugs trying to do business. Another hour remained before the real work began of tearing down and packing the rides and games and grab-your-food joints. Loud hip-hop music poured from the speakers, heavy beats resonating in Zane's bones. Tiffany was tipsy, swept up in the music and dancing by herself. Lettie and Angel fed each other pieces of funnel cake, powdered sugar coating their hands. Bingo watched Kayleigh gyrate with a gigantic stuffed unicorn she'd won—or taken—from one of the game booths. Zane looked around for Gene, thinking a fight might kick up between the two over Kayleigh's attention, but the man was nowhere to be found. That probably wasn't good.

Zane walked over to the port-a-potty area to see if he could spot Gene or the two FBI agents when the shit literally hit. A black pick-up truck—one of those huge ones—jumped the curb to the park and came barreling down the grass, leaving clouds of dust. Bright headlights with a bluish tinge, the custom kind, and darkened windows kept the driver out of view. It sped past Zane and the port-a-potties, clipping one on the side. Zane watched as the toilet spilled to its side, blue chemicals spilling out through the open door. Gene wasn't in that port-a-john, he thought with some disappointment.

"What the hell? What the hell?" Bingo ran after the truck as it drove toward the back of the park, where the office trailer was parked. Agents Oliphant and Strom followed, guns drawn. "FBI," Strom shouted.

"FBI?" Tiffany mouthed at Zane, her eyes wide. He didn't

know what to say to her so he just shrugged, leaving her to draw her own conclusions about why they had been talking to an FBI agent. But the black truck half the crowd was running toward wasn't the only thing menacing on the carnival grounds. From the park's south end, Zane saw another car jump the curb, going fast, then braking hard. This one was a dark-colored SUV but with no tint in the windows shielding the driver and passenger from view. Or the snouts of the two automatic weapons that they had resting in their laps. The kinds of guns that soldiers carry, but they didn't look like they were coming to save the day. It stopped and waited.

"Strom, over there!" He shouted but she didn't hear him over the dense beats of a rap song about money and guns. "Someone turn this music off!"

"The controls are back there," Angel said, pointing to where the truck and the SUV had converged by the cluster of trailers used for office functions.

Zane scanned the crowd, taking some deep breaths. Adrenalin and fear pricked hard as he fought down panic. He reminded himself he had been in danger before. He'd made it through before.

"Oh no no no no!" Bingo said. "Zane, come with me!" He ran ahead without looking back to see if Zane was following, toward the storage trailers and the men with guns. Zane hesitated.

"My mom is back there!" Angel said.

Zane's hesitation turned into a deep freeze. Whatever was going on here was not going to end well and the wisest move would be to get Lettie out of here. But the fear on Angel's face made him remember how it felt when he lost his mother in the fire. He would have done anything to save her. Angel must feel the same.

"Text her then call her," he said. "Tell her to get down and not come out. Or maybe she should run. I don't know. But make sure she knows what's coming."

Angel's fingers flew over the phone screen as he sent the message.

"Is this why the police were here? Because something was going to go down?" Tiffany's voice was low and excited.

"I don't know," Zane said.

Maxine emerged from the palm reading tent looking like a belly dancer ready to do the dance of a thousand scarves. Wispy pieces of fabric, some with tassels, hung from her like cobwebs.

"Now would be the time for some protective magic," Zane said to her. He knew it was a stupid joke but his mind was casting around for any kind of plan.

Maxine raised her eyebrows. "Now's the time for getting out while the getting is good. Come on, Tiffany. We should leave."

"Zane, what do you think?"

It was a good question, Zane thought. For him, the choice was clear that he had to stay and see this play out. But he felt just one small bit safer because he knew at least two FBI agents were on site, maybe more. And with Gene here, it seemed like something big was going down. Maybe this would be their ticket out.

But he still didn't know what to say to Tiffany.

"Maybe you should go with Maxine," he said, but her eyes told him that was the wrong answer. "Or just stay with us. We're not leaving yet."

Maxine looked all around. First toward the two vehicles parked at angles near the three trailers that served as the carnival headquarters, and then at the crowd, which had separated into two groups. Bystanders like them, clustered together, some with cell phone cameras raised, watching from afar. The other group, including Oliphant, Strom and Bingo, approached the two vehicles. The FBI agents moved slowly, carefully. Bingo's movements were wild, erratic. He turned around and glared at Zane, waving him to come toward him.

"Protective magic can't help you if you don't get yourself out of danger," Maxine said.

"Sometimes you have to run toward it," Zane said.

Someone finally turned off the music and in its place came a weird hushed silence, just low murmurs coming from the crowd. Underneath that was the growling hum of the diesel generators running the lights. "Stay here," he said to Lettie and Angel.

"I want to go see if my mother is okay," Angel said. "She's not answering my texts."

"I'll go see, okay?" Zane wanted to get down there, not so much to help Bingo, but to find out what was going on and whether or not this surprise ambush was somehow connected to the identity theft ring. He figured he was safe enough with the phalanx of police present and the two FBI agents.

He ran the same path Bingo had taken, down the center of the midway, through the rides and past the backs of the game stands and refreshment shacks, past the Ferris wheel.

Two men jumped out of the SUV. They were carrying guns like a commando team and their appearance sent an electrical current through the crowd, a mix of adrenalin and excitement and fear so palpable Zane could smell it. He looked for Oliphant and Strom but didn't see them.

Zane finally reached Bingo's side. "What are they after?"

"My other business," Bingo said. "It's a partnership dispute."

Zane scanned the crowd for Mike Rooke and found Bingo's

partner just ten feet away, squinting at the spectacle just as they were.

"You don't mean Mike, do you?"

Bingo shook his head.

"What's their end game here?"

"Not sure. Suicide maybe?"

The outcome didn't look promising to Zane. Bingo's partners came in strong with the element of surprise and caught them all flat-footed. Two more men exited the truck and the blond spikes could only mean one person: Gene.

"You're partners with that guy in the strip club?"

"Nah," Bingo replied. "Something else." Zane's heart ticked faster than a clock, two beats to every second. Partners with Gene but not in the strip club. What else could it be but the credit card stealing business? All along, Bingo must have known why Wally Zittman died, who Kevin Perrine was, what Lettie was doing. Why she left Tulsa for Los Angeles. Did he also know why she came back?

"He's an idiot." Bingo was perfectly still but Zane could feel the emotions and adrenalin coming off of him like a wave as he seemed to be trying to work out his next move. "Brought a lot of trouble right to our doorstep."

A breeze picked at their hair and the loose fabric of Zane's shirt, blowing hope into the deeper reaches of his mind the same way it gathered loose leaves and litter and swept it away. Knowing this connection meant that the FBI was closer than ever to breaking up the credit card ring and freeing his sister from her obligations to them.

"What can I do to help?" Zane said. "Should I call the police?" He hesitated to mention that he knew of two FBI agents on site.

"Not yet. I just need to make sure no one goes in that trailer." Bingo pointed at the trailer the four gunmen now surrounded. It was the one that housed the accountant and the woman who dispensed rolls of tickets. Zane had been inside it a few times. It was kept cold, full of benches and racks, drooping wires and boxes, six or so laptops lined up side-by-side. A tall tower with blinking lights. It had reminded him of the IT rooms at the zoo and he'd never thought to question why a traveling carnival would need that kind of IT. He just figured Bingo liked his tech. After all, he was always fiddling around on his own laptop. But now, he could not believe he had missed it.

The identity theft ring had been right here all the time. The servers and laptops that Oliphant and Strom asked them to keep an eye out for were right in front of them. And it was a smart idea too, a traveling crime network and carnival, moving from town to town. Zane had heard Mike Rooke refer to the carnival's customers as "marks" sometimes, meaning people who were easily fooled into spending their money. The term took on an even more sinister point as Zane thought of the thousands of people targeted through the ring. You could call it a victimless crime because the banks bore the brunt of the financial risk but that didn't mean it had no toll on the victims.

The black truck backed up to the hitch of the accountant's trailer and Bingo started running, his steel-toe boots raising small puffs of red-brown dust from the weed-patched ground. Two gunman stood on either side of the hitch as another guided the truck into position. Zane realized Bingo was worried about the wrong thing. The men weren't here to go inside the trailer. They were here to steal it.

Bingo got within twenty feet of Gene before the man held up a gun and aimed at him. Everyone froze.

"Stay right there," Gene shouted. He had the gun aimed low, right at Bingo's stomach.

"We can work this out," Bingo said. "Let's talk."

"Just stand back and let us get what we came here for. No one has to get hurt."

Then came a tremendous gunshot explosion and a harsh bang as a bullet hit a tree as a warning. The crowd of looky-loos let out a collective gasp and half of them had the foresight to drop to the ground, out of the way of gunfire. A few fools continued filming.

Strom stepped out and said "FBI. Stay where you are."

Oliphant emerged on the opposite side of the carnival headquarters, leveled his gun at Gene and repeated the line. Zane watched as Gene and his three goons glanced at both agents, calculating their risk. Gene kept his gun on Bingo.

"Drop the guns and raise your hands," Strom said, her voice as loud as a bullhorn.

At first, Zane thought it was working. The four guys were calculating their odds. Gene seemed stunned, thrown off his game. Zane enjoyed seeing it.

Then he realized that Strom and Oliphant were alone. No other FBI agents or police officers were emerging. Had they called for back-up? Was anyone on the way? The agents had the element of surprise on their side but that advantage was evaporating with every second. He hoped they had a plan better than shouting "drop your guns."

"What if we don't?" Gene said with a more than a flicker of anger and aggression. The other men shifted their stances, ready for a fight. "Change in plans," he said to the two men by the trailer hitch. "Grab the computers inside."

One man tried the door and to everyone's surprise it swung open easy. From inside, a woman's voice cried out "Please don't hurt me!"

The second man followed him in and came out again with a stack of laptops, black and silver. Lots of them. The other man followed him out with a similar set.

Bingo took a step toward Gene, who laughed and pointed with his gun. "Come on then," he said. "I'll meet you halfway with a bullet."

"This is nothing. I'll just move on, that's all. One door closes, another opens," Bingo said.

The wail of police sirens coming closer was the happiest tune Zane had ever heard. Out of the corner of his eye he saw the flashing lights of the patrol cars as they hopped the curb and came to rest ten yards out, headlights spotlighting Bingo and the men. Their eyes were as wide as rats caught in the kitchen at midnight, and one of them dropped his gun and started running, fast and hard toward the street. A patrol car just arriving made a sharp U-turn and followed him.

"Drop your gun," Strom shouted again. "Get on the ground."

This time, Gene did what she said. It was over. Zane turned around, searching the crowd until he saw Lettie, Angel and Tiffany, huddled together by the Tilt-a-Whirl ride. Their faces were pale, but they were safe.

When Agents Oliphant and Strom knocked on the apartment door on Monday morning, Zane and Lettie were looking at infant car seats to buy online. The amount of stuff that babies needed was astounding and expensive, Zane thought. He wasn't sure how they would make it work, other than how they always made things work. One step at a time.

He rose from the sunken cushions of the sofa. It was like coming out of quicksand but they couldn't afford a new one anytime soon, and the piece of plywood he'd added to try to steady the frame only served to make it more uncomfortable. He opened the door and let them in.

"Want to sit down?" He gestured toward the chairs

surrounding the kitchen table, where breakfast dishes still sat with the remnants of the morning's meal of frozen waffles.

"We're not going to be that long," Strom said. "We have some good news for you."

"Let's hear it."

Lettie put her phone face down on the sofa. "Don't mind me if I don't get up," she said.

"Stay where you are. No worries."

"You all got lucky," Oliphant said. He looked unhappy about their good fortune for some reason. "That trailer that Gene was trying to steal? That was the smoking gun for us. The laptops and the servers that the identity theft ring was using were all in there."

Zane and Lettie were quiet a long moment. Zane had certainly hoped that was the case but hearing it from the agents could only mean one thing.

"You don't need me anymore as an informant or a witness?" Lettie said. "All that evidence will hold up in court and all that?"

"We basically have the whole enterprise laid out on those laptops. The only thing better would be a formal confession and from the way Gene, Bingo and Mike are turning on one another, I suspect we will get one of them to crack eventually."

Lettie gazed up at Oliphant and Strom. "Thank you," she said. "You don't know how much this means to me."

"We have an idea," Strom said.

"Like I said, you got lucky," Oliphant said, compelled to have the last word. "You may be called to testify but for now, you're done with us."

Relief blew through Zane like a warm wind. They had done it. Lettie was done with this.

Zane shut the door behind the departing agents and turned to find Lettie out of the couch and right behind him, her arms stretched out. She fell into him, her face pressed into his shoulder and he wrapped his arms around her. He didn't know how much he needed that embrace until her arms wrapped around him and her head rested on his shoulder. He had a sudden feeling of peace, as everything in the universe was not just connected, it was in harmony.

And so, if this life in front of them with a baby on the way was not the life he would have chosen for his sister, what did it matter? Here they were, together.

"I can't believe it's over," she said. The regret in her voice made Zane's heart ache to comfort her. He and Lettie may be a mess of a family but brighter days were ahead. He knew it.

"Now we just have to focus on what's next for you. School. Baby. Graduation. College. Most importantly, no more crime."

She backed out of the hug. "Jeez, Zane, ever heard of enjoying the moment?"

"I'm just taking advantage of you listening to me for once."

He had a sudden thought of his mother when she found out she was pregnant with him. She had been a few years older than Lettie, but what plans had their mother put aside to create space for him in her life? Some people get to cross all the adult milestones in some traditional order: college degree, good job, savings account, house and mortgage, marriage, babies. He'd always known he was different. He had hoped Lettie would find her way more easily. But who could say which way of life was best for anyone?

Ernest had been right, as usual. Zane and Lettie had to find their own stories. How had he put it? Something about turning off the phones and the television and feeling the wind on your skin, the weight of a pebble between your fingertips. So many of the stories they told themselves came from advertisers trying to sell them stuff. So much so that people like Emmaline created their own false sets of stories online. Stories that bore no resemblance to their real lives.

Lettie would find her own story in her own time. Keeping the baby was her choice and she would make it work and he would help her in every way he could. But he had to start living his own story and he knew what he should do. Helping people was his true north. He would apply to the police academy.

Chapter Thirty-Nine

Zane was sunning on a patch of grass at River West Park, enjoying an energy slushee drink concoction from QuikTrip called Kiss the Rooster, when his phone dinged with a text message from Emmaline's dad.

"We're having a welcome home party for Emmaline," Cy Perryman wrote. "Come by if you can."

The party was in a few days, organized almost as quickly as she had decided to leave Los Angeles. He had used the confetti and balloon emojis in the message to convey his joy at his daughter's return. Zane hadn't thought Cy knew what emojis were. Cy had already expressed his gratitude to Zane for helping bring his daughter home. That visit-turned-intervention that Lettie, Angel and he had made planted the seeds, Emmaline had said.

"The prodigal daughter comes home," Zane said, turning the phone screen face-down on the grass.

Tiffany, who was scrolling through videos on her phone beside him, glanced up.

"What's that?"

"Emmaline's parents are throwing a party to welcome her home."

Tiffany narrowed her eyes at him. "Your ex-girlfriend, eh?"

"She was never my girlfriend," Zane said. "And she's more like family."

"Kissing cousins, maybe," Tiffany said, the two words sliding into one another *kissincuzzins* in her slightly country accent just like a kiss.

"Come with me then," he said. "Let me show you off at the Majestic Trailer Park."

"So romantic. A return date to where we met. And a chance to meet your former, uh, flame."

"Your choice," he said, grinning because he knew she would come.

The energy of the afternoon was sleepy and restful. Even the group of bicycle-riding men dressed in gaudy spandex billboarded with company names couldn't affect it. Further out, the Arkansas River glittered under the sun like the smooth skin of the catfish swimming in its murky waters.

"They finally got the carnival rides and trailers off of the Eastside Mall parking lot," Zane said, shielding his eyes from the sun's sharp reflection on the water. He picked up a tiny seed pod that had fallen from one of the trees and tossed it toward the river.

"Moving on to the next town?"

"No, like in some federal impound or something. With Bingo and Mike Rook arrested for their roles in the identity theft ring, their assets were seized as evidence. Dozens of people lost their jobs."

"Wow. Crime doesn't pay."

Zane grimaced. "I have to make sure Lettie truly learned that lesson."

"I think she did." Tiffany put the phone on her leg and ran her hand up and down his arm. His skin sparked to life under her fingertips, raising the hairs on the back of his neck in a wave of pleasure.

"I talked to a friend of mine who works at TechSquad, you know that company that sends people out to fix computer problems? They might have a job for Lettie."

"Really? That's amazing," Zane said. Someone in AA had read a quote from some old German writer named Goethe the other day. It resonated so much with him that he found it on the internet and printed it out to hang in the kitchen. The part he loved said, "...the moment one definitely commits oneself, then Providence moves too. All sorts of things occur to help one that would never have otherwise occurred." For him, Verda's decision to move to Tulsa to help take care of the baby while Lettie and Angel finished school fell into that miraculous category. And he'd taken the rest of that quote to heart too with his application to the police academy: "Whatever you can do, or dream you can do, begin it."

"I'd hire her myself at the store, but it just doesn't look right to hire my boyfriend's sister. Nepotism and all," Tiffany said.

The hairs on the back of his neck did their flip and shiver thing again.

"I'm your boyfriend?"

"I hope so," Tiffany said.

He wrapped his arm around her and pulled her in close to capture her lips with his. The kiss was a new chapter beginning, one full of promise and hope, with a woman who truly saw him for who he was.

When he pulled back to look at her, he whispered, "I'm so happy I found you."

Tiffany shook her head and laughed. "I found you, silly."

Every one of us has a thread running through our lives, Ernest had told him. A trajectory that slowly arcs toward the good. The *ouroboros* reminding us destruction leads to rebirth again and again.

He felt the thread connecting him and Tiffany, him and Lettie, Angel, Verda, Ernest. Gerry and Chris and Maxine. The miracle and magic of family and faith and service advancing through cycles of ends and beginnings. He couldn't wait to see what happened next.

Preview of Stalked By Revenge

STALKED BY REVENGE

Chapter 1
Zane

All Good Things Must

"I've been shot! I need an ambulance!"

The dash-cam footage was black-and-white and grainy, but the audio filled the classroom with crystal clarity. A man's voice, rough with pain, screamed for help into his radio as tail-lights sped away.

Watching the videos of police officers being ambushed and killed was a weekly ritual in Cal Himmelman's class. Zane Clearwater hated it. Six weeks into Oklahoma's consolidated police training, the videos had gotten easier to watch but the first three shook him to the core. He had seen enough people die up close and personal: his father Jeremiah Doom and that poor sod Wally Zittman at the carnival. Every violent death took him back to the trauma of his father. Two years later, he had just gotten better at moving past it.

Who was he kidding, Zane thought. The videos didn't get easier to watch. And it didn't get any easier to listen to Himmelman's commentary either.

"Situations change in a heartbeat," Himmelman said. "You're being watched constantly. You can be getting a cup of coffee like that guy was, and people take your measure. Calculate their odds, especially in anti-police neighborhoods like they got in Oklahoma City and Tulsa. Heck, even out in some small towns, there are blocks where you don't know who's watching and who has a gun. It's us against them."

Zane slumped against the hard back of the chair-desk combo. This mentality made him feel like an outsider. He'd been faced with murder charges when his mother died in a mysterious fire and without the help of Detective Angus Pastor, he might have been convicted. He wanted to be a police officer who helped people, not one who wore suspicion like a second skin. He wasn't sure there was a place for him in law enforcement some days.

"Not everyone without a badge is a criminal." The voice came from behind him, but Zane did not have to turn around to know who said it. Devante Flores constantly argued with the instructor and the classmates who bought into the us-versus-them mentality.

"That's true enough," said Himmelman. "But you never know. People are unpredictable. When you walk up to a house to investigate a noise complaint, you don't know who is behind that door and what weapon they have. You've got to be looking for your escape route if things go to hell."

Most of the class nodded along with Himmelman, fully invested. The handful that had hesitations or felt the same as Devante sat quiet.

No bells rang, but Himmelman must have had something better to do because he glanced at the clock and said the magic words. Zane slipped his notebook and pen into his backpack slowly. He was in no hurry to get to the mini boxing matches that were next on the schedule.

Zane scrolled through the text thread from his sixteen-year-old sister Lettie this morning, re-examining the latest sonogram of his niece in utero. So many hopes and dreams came with that little peanut of a person, curled tight. The baby was a surprise for their family, and he certainly hadn't wanted his baby sister to get pregnant at such a young age, but he'd never call this baby unwanted. He planned to give little peanut and his sister everything he never had and then some. This job with the Skiatook police department was going to make that possible.

The booming voice of Scott, one of their cohort's loudest and most aggressive members, interrupted his thoughts. "Maybe you should have gone to social work school," Scott said, directing his derision at Devante as he often did. His towering frame bumped into Zane as he and his two friends headed for the classroom door, pausing one-by-one to kick at Devante's black boots to mar the glossy shine required for inspections. They laughed and slapped one another's backs like they'd just made comedy gold.

"What a bunch of assholes," Devante said. He bent to pick his notebook and pen from the floor by his desk as the classroom cleared out.

"Maybe you can land some punches during the boxing matches," Zane said. He felt sorry for Devante, but Devante stood in his own way a lot of the time. The dude had a lot to learn about picking his battles and finding the right time to make his arguments. But Zane could appreciate a hothead. He had those tendencies himself and worked hard to control them. But he could still remember going off on Randy Womack, his old boss at the Tulsa Zoo, and getting fired.

"Not likely. I really don't think those guys understand what going fifty percent means." He was referring to the defensive tactics instructor's admonition that during the boxing matches, the fighters should only exert half of the power they would during a real fight. "Someone's gonna get hurt."

Devante was shorter than most of the class, and in his place, Zane would probably shy away from hand-to-hand combat too. A former high school wrestler, Devante possessed some skills, but mostly after the fight had gone to the ground.

Zane stood up from his seat and glanced at his phone again, surprised to see a voicemail notification pop-up. A call must have come through in the few moments since he had last looked at it. They were supposed to keep their phones in their lockers at the academy, but most ignored that order but kept them on silent all day.

He knew it was Old Spice before even really looking because no one else in his life would leave a voicemail. Not even his grandmother did it anymore, saying she preferred texts because he always answered faster.

He listened for a few seconds as Old Spice identified himself as though caller ID didn't exist and then got to the news the Tulsa police detective had called to deliver.

His heart dropped.

"Clyde Doom could get out of prison," the detective said. "I wanted you to know as soon as I heard."

Zane pressed the phone closer to his ear as though it would somehow block the words from entering the world. Just when he thought he and Lettie were safe and on the right track. *Clyde.*

"You coming?" said Devante. Zane stood immobile in the classroom for a few beats longer, then forced himself to move.

"Yeah, right behind you," he said.

The instructor met Zane's eyes across the classroom as Devante exited. "Everything all right? You look like you saw a ghost." Himmelman's observation skills outshined his people skills every day of the week.

Zane shuddered at the memories dredged up by hearing Clyde's name. Acne-cheeked Clyde, Zane's youngest half-brother, usually glassy-eyed from meth. The blotchy, shaky-lined wolf tattoo on his neck. The gun in his hand. Lettie tied up.

He felt trapped. He wanted to get out the classroom, walk out of the building, go to Lettie and keep her safe. He managed a few faltering steps toward the door, frozen by foreboding mixed with anger. How was this happening?

Himmelman ran his meaty hand over his balding head and sighed. They were alone in the classroom now and the sound from the hallways had died down as well. Everyone was moving out to the gym.

"I'm not trying to be an asshole, Clearwater. I'm trying to be the little voice in your head that says, 'be careful or you can die out there.' This is a serious job with serious consequences. Not everyone makes it home at the end of their shift."

His words rang true in a way Zane hadn't reckoned with before, but not the way Himmelman meant them.

"I get it," Zane said truthfully. And Himmelman didn't have to try to be an asshole. He made it a lifestyle.

Zane forced his legs to move out of the classroom and toward the building exit, two glass doors emptying onto the winter-white quad. Panic scraped at his stomach. He slowed his breath, counting to five before exhaling it in a visible puff to alleviate his growing fear. As he headed toward the gym behind one or two stragglers, the afternoon sun slipped behind clouds, erasing his shadow. Behind him, he heard the clang and thwack as the wind whipped up the American and Oklahoma State flags on the flagpole at the training center.

Zane hit the call-back button on his phone, finger shaking.

"Zane," Old Spice said.

"How is this possible?"

"The appellate court overturned his conviction and twenty-year sentence. Said the trial judge was sexually harassing the district attorney who prosecuted the case."

"What does that mean?"

Old Spice's gruff voice took on an edgy tone. "It means he gets a new trial. But it also means he might be getting out on bail while he waits for a federal trial because of that McGirt ruling. He's part Cherokee, just like you, and the crime happened in Indian Country when he was a juvenile. Everything's backlogged in the U.S. Attorney's office so who knows when that will happen."

"Is he out now?" Zane said. His voice was hard and clipped and felt like it rose from an anger that threatened to consume him.

"Not yet," Old Spice said. "Now there's a good chance they'll keep him locked up until that new trial. But you never know."

Zane pushed through the front doors of the gym, the smell of floor polish and sweaty socks assaulting his nostrils. The cold air outside had chilled the thin layer of perspiration on his arms and neck, another sign his anxiety still rocketed. His emotions cycled through denial, rage, fear, and finally settled on the numbness of shock. It would be so easy to run. Probably smarter too. But distance wouldn't deter Clyde's vengeance. And fleeing would just delay the inevitable.

Maybe he wouldn't have to stand his ground. Maybe Clyde would toe the straight line and not try to seek revenge for Zane killing their father and testifying against Clyde and his brother Link in their trial.

Yeah, and maybe Lettie was going to give birth to a magic unicorn.

He changed his clothes and entered the practice gym. A crowd of trainees surrounded a makeshift boxing ring made of crime scene tape and stacked traffic cones. Cue Zane's internal eyeroll. The academy had enough money for a real boxing ring setup. This makeshift one was the defensive arts instructor's idea of a joke. And there was Ryan, standing in the middle of the room like a hillbilly sensei, his tan felt cowboy hat shading his eyes and his short grey mustache and beard. An enormous key ring hung off his belt like an old-fashioned jailer's ring. A few pairs of trainees around him sparred with smiles on their faces, more light-hearted than Zane felt. Laughter and mainly male voices bounced around the high-ceilinged gym, though about ten women were in their cohort. The women tended to take the trainings more seriously, Zane had noticed.

On the far side of the room, two women in the academy's black berets, T-shirts and loose pants engaged in one-on-one combat on blue mats, a snap punch and high knee rise blocked. A few of the instructors hung out on the gymnasium bleachers to watch the show, passing a bag of chips. Zane saw Turner, the copper-headed firearms instructor, glance at him and look away again. Turner said something to the other instructors, who each looked at Zane and back again. Maybe the news of Clyde's good fortune and Zane's bad luck traveled fast. Everyone in the academy knew about Zane's past.

"Gather round, people," Ryan said. He was slow on his feet and in the way he talked, but he had a sharpshooter's eye for creating dramatic match-ups. He must have heard the news about Clyde, too, because he called out Zane's name for the first match. Probably thought he was doing Zane a favor by giving him an outlet for his anger.

Fine, Zane thought, grabbing a fresh mouthpiece from Ryan and letting the man lace him into gloves.

"Against Zane today we'll have Big Scott," the instructor said. Zane wavered and sucked his teeth. Scott, the jerk he'd just seen bullying Devante in class, was not just bigger than he was. He was also a dirty fighter, making a hobby of terrorizing weaker trainees.

Scott's posse of smaller bullies stomped their feet and clapped for him. "He'll knock you out at twenty percent!"

"Three minutes," Ryan said. "Don't give it all you got. Just half-effort, got it?"

Scott winked at him, a big comic wink as though mugging for television cameras on one of those old comedy shows with a laugh track. The urge to smack that stupid expression off his face intensified, and he hopped over the crime scene tape, soft blue mats under his feet. Maybe throwing some punches was the right medicine for the moment. And if Big Scott bested him, fine. He had taken plenty of punches in his life; he could take a few more.

Ryan rang the bell. Zane went in fast with a first punch, no time for dancing and ducking. The men traded attacks, Scott's right hook sending Zane reeling. If Big Scott was operating at fifty percent, Zane didn't want to see what his full capacity looked like. He was throwing punches without mercy, a hard look in his eyes. Zane absorbed the punches and let Clyde's face superimpose itself over Scott's sweaty one. Clyde coming for him. Clyde coming for Lettie. No one to stop him. Zane jabbed at Scott's face as if bashing his way out of a burning building. It felt good to let go of some of that anger.

At the end of the three minutes, Zane had fended off the attacks and counterattacks and left Big Scott panting and surprised. He liked being underestimated and wanted to hold on to the feeling of satisfaction that came from surprising an opponent, but the fight had been a hard one and his energy was spent. Getting hit in the head can rattle your brain, he thought. But something in Scott's eyes, that hard meanness, had reminded him of the cruelty of his father and half-brothers. Even on the right side of the law, the capacity for meanness and injustice existed. It was human nature but it also depressed him.

"Good fight, men," Ryan said. "But I think that was more than half-effort. Next match-up, I need you to take that order seriously."

"I did hold back," Scott muttered to Zane as he crossed the mat. "You piece-of-shit lowlife. You don't belong here."

Scott's words were pure loser's bluster, Zane reminded himself, shaking his head as though to loosen them from his brain. He headed for the water fountain, managing a smile or two for Devante and a few of the others who clapped him on the back as though he'd won some title match-up. He didn't want to watch the rest of the fights, but the instructors would expect him to.

He took a deep breath, remembering his resolve. Nothing was going to keep him from his goal of helping people find justice. Nothing. The resolve had grown in him since he had faced the terror of being wrongfully accused of killing his mother, and he was more determined than ever to become a part of the law enforcement community. He had overcome the odds to get hired as an officer-in-training by the Skiatook Police Department, one of the handful of cities that didn't require college coursework, which he didn't have. He had landed in this training program and fought daily to keep his place. His instructors said he had potential and lauded his hard work. But this wasn't just about getting top grades or showing these idiots he wasn't a quitter or not disappointing Old Spice, who had vouched for him.

This was about learning every single skill he could to become a person who could really help people who needed it. Someone who understood the right and the wrong side of the law and could help good people navigate the grey areas in between.

And today, with the news about Clyde, it was about protecting himself, Lettie, and the baby from danger. Again.

With everyone's attention on another match-up in the ring, Zane bent down to grab the backpack he'd left on one of the low bleachers and unzipped the front pocket. Breaking the news to Lettie about Clyde would be best done in person, but he wouldn't get out of training until after nine o'clock this evening. So the phone would have to do.

"I just heard about that criminal who kidnapped your sister getting a new trial," said Cal Himmelman. Zane startled at his voice. The stocky instructor certainly could walk on cat's feet when he didn't want to be noticed. His appearance over Zane's right shoulder felt like an ambush.

"If it's not that McGirt verdict tying our hands, it's good convictions that don't stand because of some technicality," he said. The name McGirt was shorthand for the landmark Supreme Court case decision that held that much of eastern Oklahoma was Indian land. The Supreme Court's ruling complicated how the state could prosecute criminal cases on Indian land and between people of Indian heritage.

Zane and his half-brothers shared Cherokee blood, but to Zane the ruling seemed like an abstraction, something for the powers-that-be to sort out. He wasn't sure how to even think about it. And anyway, it wasn't why Clyde had gotten a break. A judge who couldn't treat his female co-workers with respect was the reason. Crazy, unintended consequences of #MeToo.

"You're one of us, now, Clearwater. Don't forget that,"

Himmelman said. "We've got your back just like you've got ours, okay?"

Zane didn't feel the connection, really. Himmelman's statement of support came with qualifiers. Everything was a loyalty test. Everything was about creating an us-versus-them mentality that just didn't ring true for all the grey areas Zane knew existed. Still, he needed allies and he wasn't about to alienate Himmelman.

"I appreciate that," he said.

"There's people here who'll help you. You just got to ask. I know Angus Pastor thinks highly of you, and for some of us that's enough."

Zane wondered where that sympathy and support had been for all the weeks leading up to this moment.

"Good," he said. "It's a lot to process right now. I think I'm in shock."

Zane saw the calculation in the other man's eyes. Himmelman sized him up one more time then pressed a business card into Zane's hand.

"My personal cell is on here," he said. "You call me if anything comes up. If you have any questions or anything. I'm retired now and I might be more helpful to you then you think."

It was an oddly cryptic thing for a straightshooter like Himmelman to say and Zane wasn't sure what to make of it. He ran his finger along the edge of the card. The edges were bent and softened as though the card had sat in a wallet for years without use. He couldn't imagine a world in which he would call Himmelman for help, but he thanked him again for it and slipped it into the cargo pocket of his pants. He reflexively pulled out his phone to glance at the screen only to be surprised by seeing Lettie's name and face on the screen. She was video calling him. Himmelman tapped the side of his nose. "You oughta take that, I'm guessing," he said. "Even though it's against the rules, I think most will give you a pass today based on what's going on."

Indeed, word had travelled fast through the law enforcement grapevine.

"Zane, can you come home?" Lettie said. Her face was visible only momentarily, in fragments, as she walked through the mobile home Verda had bought for them at the newly renamed Majestic Mobile Home and RV Park in Tulsa. On Zane's phone screen appeared one of Lettie's eyes, opened wide, eyebrow arched. Then her lips, pressed together tight. Then the white ceiling fan turning slowly. Zane's stomach clenched and panic throttled his breathing. Dread descended like a thick fog, making his bones feel leaden, unmanageable. It was Friday morning, and police academy cadets were prohibited from leaving the campus until dismissal at six in the evening.

"What's going on?"

"It's all over Twitter," she said. "Clyde Doom is getting out of prison."

"I was just going to call to tell you," he said.

"But something weird happened. This package came." The phone camera swept to a white plastic envelope. A yellow baby rattle shaped like a lion's head smiled back at Zane.

"Adorable," Zane said, relief slowing his heart even as confusion replaced it. Why would Lettie call him about this?

"It just appeared on the doorstep an hour ago," she said, her eyes widening with fear. "No return address, no card, nothing. A baby rattle in a white envelope with my name on it."

"One of your friends maybe?" Zane said. "A rogue Amazon delivery?"

Hand shaking, she held the camera over the white envelope. Only her name was on it, no address.

"Not from Amazon. And I checked with my friends. I called Maxine at Earth Spells, I checked with Emmaline and her parents, I spoke with Dock Hirsch across the way, I even called Angel's mom. No one dropped a baby rattle off here. Plus, me and Verda have been here all day. A friend would have just knocked at the door." Her words spun faster and faster, reminding Zane of the carnival's gravity ride, spinning so fast that the floor could fall away and riders would be pinned to the walls. He felt pinned to the wall.

"Calm down," Zane said even though he felt nothing like calm inside. "Has anyone been in touch with you recently on social? Anyone who could have just found out you were pregnant? Maybe there's an easy explanation for this. Magnolia, maybe?"

But as soon as he thought of his ex-girlfriend, he remembered her latest post about a new job in St. Louis. Anyway, she had known about Lettie's pregnancy and even donated to his sister's GoFundMe campaign.

"I guess I didn't check with Tiffany, but why would she leave it on the doorstep?"

Hearing his current girlfriend's name brought her face and smile into his mind, a sweet pause in an anxiety-filled day. "Doesn't make sense. She'd be coming over this weekend anyway," Zane said. "One of Verda's friends? What's the name of that man who moved into the place with the carport covered in chicken wire? The one who kind of flirts with Verda?"

"Leon something? I guess I could walk over there and ask," she said. "But Zane, what if it's Clyde somehow? And he knows where we live?"

Lettie's worried face filled the screen, the look in her eyes taking him back to the moment when he saw her tied up and terrified in the Dooms' compound in those insane weeks following his mother's death. The decision he made to pull the trigger on his father, Jeremiah Doom. It was the only decision he could have made. But it was also one that haunted him like an unfriendly ghost every day since. And now the specter had come to life with his half-brother Clyde Doom possibly walking free.

"He's still in prison right now, so it wasn't him directly. Let's take it one step at a time," Zane said. "It's weird all right and it's hard to overlook the timing, but maybe there's a simple explanation for this." He took a deep breath and started to fill Lettie in on what little information he had heard from Old Spice. What he didn't need to tell her was that he would protect her at all cost. She already knew that.

Acknowledgments

My most sincere thanks to:

Kayla Harris for holding me accountable to finishing this sequel and inspiring me with the wild, amazing creativity of her writing about post-apocalyptic motorcycle gangs, mermaids on Catalina Island, and haunted English manor houses.

Editor Susan Krawitz for helping me find Zane's true north through her insightful and sensitive review.

My mother Rosemary Lipinski and my sister Laura Kane for their unwavering and enthusiastic support of my writing.

My husband Stephen Arakawa for always believing in me.

The amazing TikTok community of #booktok #indieauthortok that reignited my love of books and writing.